IN THE WIND

stories

by

Peter Breschard

IN THE WIND

Some stories have appeared in
PINDELDYBOZ, THE FICTION WAREHOUSE,
and THE PEDESTAL MAGAZINE

also by Peter Breschard
DEAD LEPERS
IMELDA AND FRIENDS

Published by Galldubh Press
Okemos, Michigan
galldubh@aol.com

ISBN: 978-0-6151-4231-9

Printed in the United States of America

BREAKFAST SERVICES
AT BARB'S DINER

"Hey, these numbers can't be right." Phil steps up to the counter as he inspects the stats one more time. "No way, not for a kid his age."

"Some kids got it. Some don't. He's got it. He's got a lot of it." George rearranges scrambled eggs on his plate. "They'll gobble him up in no time flat. Probably be playing the Bigs before he's eighteen."

Phil waves down the woman working behind the counter then parks his butt on a stool next to his partner. She moves into position, and braces both men. "Barb, hey, how's 'bout some of your excellent waffles this fine morning?" Nodding, she scribbles notes in her pad. "Coffee, one of these bad boys," he points out a particular cruller beneath a plastic dome perched on the Formica counter, "and let's have some cranberry juice this morning. Hey, just for the hell of it. I'm feeling 'venturous today."

"Sure, hon." Barb rips a sheet from her pad and then impales it on the kitchen/counter passthrough spike. She slaps the bell, awakening Bernie, "The Chef". She pours Phil his java then shouts over her shoulder to the kitchen "Rise and shine, sweety pie, you can sleep when you're dead."

Bernie is moving and cooking before he's aware he's awake. He always answers the call. He tosses frozen waffles into the toaster, then sits himself down for another catnap. Dreams of southern climes and playing ball with his buddies flood Bernie's mind. He needs the rest. This isn't his only job.

"Take a kid like this guy we're talking about," George borrows Phil's newspaper. As he sips his brew, George marks notes around the article, "twenty years ago, he would've been doing what? Running cross-country?"

"Yeah, maybe baseball." Phil's half-eaten cruller rests in one hand while he brushes crumbs from the front of his zip-up jacket with the other. "Forget football, not enough meat on his bones. Forget basketball, too short. Hockey? Hey, get real. That leaves track and baseball. Yeah, cross-country or shortstop. Looks the type to me."

"And they play the damn game just about all year round. Who would have thought?"

"Here you go, hon." Barb parks a waffled filled plate and set-ups on Phil's place mat, "Anything else?"

"Hey, did I already drink my cranberry juice?"

"Sorry, Phil. You know how I get." Turning her back to the partners, Barb pours cranberry juice as she takes an order over her shoulder from a customer who's just come in and taken a seat.

"How ya doin' this mornin', hon?"

Barb delivers the order. "Happy now, Phil?"

"Couldn't be more delighted." He sips his juice. "Hey, how's your boy these days? Staying out of trouble?"

Barb's tired face lightens a bit. "Thanks for askin', hon. Who knows with kids his age? I haven't caught him at it again and the cops haven't either. So knock wood."

George motions for more coffee. "He should play sports. Keep him away from bad elements." Both George and Phil laugh. "Seriously, what's he now, thirteen, fourteen?"

"Thirteen."

"That's plenty young. Get him out of the apartment. Away from those damn computer games. Or worse. Get him out running around playing in fresh air. Supervised." George polishes off his eggs. "He like any particular sport?"

"Nothing I know anything about."

"What you mean, Barb?" Now it's Phil's turn for more coffee. "It's Spring. I know a couple of teams he might be able to play on. Hey, didn't he play Little League a couple of seasons?"

Barb rests her elbows on the counter and her head in her hands. "Forget it. He never liked baseball. The way he played, I can't blame him. He kills time watching soccer now and then. That's about as active as he gets."

Both Phil and George groan at the mention of soccer.

"Hey, Georgie, got somethin' for me?" Walking into Barb's small diner, Charlie C is all smiles.

George matches him, grin for grin. "Of course, Charlie, had yourself a good night last night. Didn't you." George looks to Phil who slides an envelope to his partner. "Who you like today?"

"Not today, Georgie. Sorry. Today I've got to cash out and run. Kids I coach need some new uniforms."

The light bulb inside the lamp Phil maintains in the recesses of his mind for illuminating brilliant ideas switches on. "Hey, still coachin' middle school, Charlie boy?"

"Yeah, Phil, ten to fourteen. I actually do some real good work with kids that age. Any older and their life's already pretty much set in stone." George hands Charlie C bills from the envelope. "Thanks, Georgie. I like workin' with kids. Keeps them from sitting in front of stupid electronic screens all day, playing video games instead of actually living."

"Not soccer is it?" Phil hopes against hope.

Charlie C cracks another grin. "Sure is, Phil, soccer. Soccer, football, whatever you want to call it." Charlie C calls out to the cook in the back. "Right, Bernardo? Football, Bernie, football. Goooooooooooal!"

From his station behind the diner's wall Bernardo chimes the call bell three times and shouts out enthusiastically, "Football!"

"Football, soccer, I don't care." Phil signals Barb, who by now has drifted off to tend other customers, to come back. "Hey, Charlie, you know Barb's kid, right?"

"Can't say I've seen him in a couple of years."

Barb joins the conversation. "Mornin', Charlie C, get ya somethin'?"

"No thanks, hon. I've got to get my rear in gear. Just now Phil mentioned your boy. Haven't seen him for a while. How's he been doin'?"

"Thanks for askin', hon. He's doin' O.K., I guess. Usual kids' stuff."

Phil catches Charlie C's eye, urging him on.

"Listen, Barb, I'm coachin' a soccer team for the parish and I need some more players. How old's the boy?"

"Thirteen."

"Perfect. How's about I give him a call later tonight and see if he wants to play on my team?"

For the first time all morning, someone smiles a smile of actual joy. "Charlie, that would be great. Let me write down the number for ya." Taking the pencil from behind her ear, Barb again scribbles in her pad. Handing the note to Charlie C, for a moment, a simple moment, their eyes meet.

Neither George nor Phil miss seeing that.

"Good man, Charlie C." George toasts him with his coffee cup. "We'll be seeing you later in the week then?"

"Sure." As Charlie C starts to leave, he looks toward Barb again and stops. "What the hell, Georgie, I'm feeling lucky this morning. Put me down for half a hundred on the Tigers."

George nods, Phil gives a quick wave, Barb's smile gets even wider, and Charlie C hits the street.

"Refills, boys? On the house." George and Phil both tap their coffee cups for more. Barb tops them off and moves on to other customers.

"Soccer. I'll never get it." George bemoans the changing times.

"So it's not our sport, George, no big deal. Adapt and move on. Hey, that's what I always say. That's my motto."

"Yeah, I guess you're right. I'll tell you one thing and it ain't two, Phil."

"What's that, George?"

"The public is never going to get the kind of service we deliver from those damn internet bookmakers. No way, no how. I'll tell you that. They can't deliver our kind of service."

"You're damn straight, George. Hey, they can't beat the personal touch."

With that, the two bookies finish their coffees. They've more work to do and other stops to make.

As the partners leave the diner, Bernie the cook awakens from another catnap dream of green fields and soccer balls.

"Goooooooooooal!!!!!"

BUGSY LANDS A SECOND LINE

Bugsy's foot is falling asleep. He shifts his weight then sends the gofer for another cup of coffee.

"Here you go, Mr. Siegel, anything else?"

The studios insist on assigning Bugsy his own flunkie whenever he's on set. None of the other people working here, except the Director, get this perk. Bugsy makes a mental note as he sips coffee and periodically shakes his foot.

"Quiet, please. Rolling."

"Ready? Action."

An electric surge shoots through Bugsy's body. Perched on a step ladder looking down on his cast and crew, the Director maintains complete control of everything and everyone about him. Bugsy's never been in such total control, even when he's forced to stick a gat in some terrified slob's ear.

"Quiet, please." That's all an assistant has to say. Two words and a hundred people shut their yaps. Shut their yaps and listen for everything. Shut their pie holes and create an active silence. Complete attention maintained by over a hundred people. Professionals coming together for one concerted effort. In silence. Such intensity.

Another surge of adrenaline kicks through Bugsy's system. What a jolt.

Too bad he didn't find this particular high earlier in life. Too bad, too late. Bugsy is what he is. On a movie sound stage such as this, the best he can hope to achieve is maybe a single line here or there. A walk-on. A cameo. And he'd only get that due to his reputation off stage, not because of any acting ability on his part.

Bugsy knows his talents. He's a thug. An extremely organized and intelligent thug. But a thug all the same. He's seen his own screen test. As an actor, he's a stiff. Bugsy knows real talent when he sees it. That's how he's survived so long in the business he's in. A man's tool may be his voice or a shiv, either way you have to appreciate workmanship. Never do something yourself when there's better talent available. Hire the best so they aren't hired by your competitors. Pay a reasonable wage and everyone gets along fine. Except, maybe, your competitors.

Bugsy's talent on set is as a background artist. Which is pretty much the same as saying he has no talent at all. He works the small crowd scenes with other members of the Union. Extras. Atmosphere artists. Like Bugsy, they have the fever to be on the screen and most have as little ability. Sure, one or two may be called up to deliver a line, now and then, but they're all either kidding themselves or in it for sheer pleasure, like Bugsy.

Keep in the back of the shot. Don't make noise. Listen to the

Director's assistant. Don't look at the camera. Be ready when they call you to the set. Not too many rules you had to know. You'd call it unskilled labor anywhere else.

And now and then an "atmosphere artist" gets a bump. Not bumped off, something else. Something special to do. Get slapped, punched, or run through by one of the principal artists. Still wouldn't say anything but it was worth extra bucks. A "bump" in the paycheck that's for sure. It means a lot to most of these people. These are the Hollywood hopeless. Biding time. Waiting for their big break. Not enough talent to land a job in front of the camera and too much ego to try for a job behind. Not that getting a job behind the camera is easier. Probably tougher. Those unions are locked solid. A tough business, no doubt about that. Bugsy loves it.

And rarely, very rarely, an extra would be asked to do something which makes them eligible to be paid as an "Actor". Two ways this happens. First way is you get recruited to say a line. The second is to be involved in a stunt. They asked Bugsy to read a line the first time he visited a set. Got his Screen Actors Guild card that day. This is one way the studio heads try to awe people with whom they are forced to do business. Put them in front of a camera and let them make fools of themselves. Didn't work with Bugsy. He read the line without fumbling. "Have another drink?" And everyone was nice to him about it. The executive showing him around made the proper soothing sounds.

Afterwards, they let Bugsy see the dailies. What they'd filmed that day. He got to watch the scene with his one line. More soothing words from more soothing executives. Bugsy sucked.

Even he could see he sucked. He tried his best. He'd been a little nervous. "Have another drink?" seemed like the easiest line in the world. His performance was flat. His voice was flat. He didn't know what to do with his face, his hands, his body.

Bugsy is a fast learner. He knew from that very moment he wasn't the next George Raft. The best he was going to be was a guest at a cocktail party where Raft has all the lines.

"Cut." The low hum of voices begins anew.

"Ben, a word if you would." Back to reality. Business before art.

Siegel nods.

"Ben, negotiations are shot to hell. Marty and I did as much as we could. They're not going to budge without more persuasion." This is Ken Somebodyorother talking to Bugsy. An executive vice-president at the Union. Marty's gofer. Standing alongside, Marty keeps quiet.

Business. Business. Business. Bugsy has enough to do without overseeing every Lilliputian detail of this operation. Why'd he get into this union racket? Sure, the money's good. But he can put his cash, time and resources into more lucrative sectors. Face facts, Bugsy tells himself almost every day, you like the work, you like the movies, that's why you're here. It's not about money. Not totally.

Bugsy watches the set's action a few moments before turning

back to the Union official.

"They're not being reasonable?"

Ken shakes his head. This time Marty Owletski speaks. "Ben, we've done everything we can do. We were thinking, maybe, you could have a word with them?" Owletski knows what he's asking.

Bugsy shrugs his shoulders. "Hold on a minute?"

Crossing the stage, Bugsy Siegel, the atmosphere artist, approaches the Director's assistant. Bugsy couldn't be nicer. "Charles, I've got to see some guys about Union business? Alright if I disappear for a couple of hours? I don't want to ruin the shot or anything?"

The kid turns and gives Bugsy the hairy eyeball for a second before he sees this isn't an ordinary scum-of-the-earth extra. The kid almost tells Bugsy Siegel, Mob Boss of Hollywood, to shut up and get back with the others.

But the Director's assistant doesn't say that to Ben Siegel. So the Director's assistant lives to a ripe old age dreaming of movies he'd make if only he were a Director.

"Sure, Mr. Siegel, whenever you come back, we'll be right here." Charles smiles and swallows hard to keep the fear in his throat from spewing out his mouth.

"Thanks."

"Ben, you ready?" Marty calls to his Boss.

Bugsy Siegel exits the stage.

"Gentlemen, you all know Mr. Benjamin Siegel, I believe?"

Bugsy never enjoys being in this kind of room. This isn't even the room where the representatives of the Union and the Studios are meeting. This is the place where the board of directors for one of the studios meets every couple of months or so. Far too ornate a venue for the nuts and bolts of real business. If the light bulbs needed changing, there would be five maintenance men rushing into the room to change them. This is where the masters meet. These guys are real pigs.

Sitting around this massive table sit a dozen or so of the Studios top men. Bugsy is familiar with most of them. He only bothers remembering the names of four or five.

After the usual preliminary noises are made, Bugsy says his piece.

"Gentlemen, up until an hour ago, I thought we'd solved our problem?" Bugsy pauses a moment for effect, he knew how to do this even before he came to Hollywood from New York. "You all know the Extras Guild won't work without a contract? Is there a problem with the Executive Branch's usual fee?"

An emphatically negative murmur flows from those perched about the table. Nobody sitting in this room is about to tell Ben "Bugsy" Siegel that they have a problem with the percentage he gets off the top. These men have wives and children and mistresses and boyfriends to support and protect. Not to mention, Bugsy makes them all a lot of money by keeping the Communists from taking over the Union. They can do business with Bugsy because Bugsy is a reasonable man. They tell him as much.

"That's what I thought? So where's the problem? It's not like we're asking the world for the rank-and-file? Is it? Is it?"

Who were the top men of the Hollywood Studios to disagree with a reasonable man like Bugsy Siegel?

"You, Mr. Mount?" Bugsy addresses one of the studio heads whose name he remembers. Mount runs one of the top five shops. Full of himself. Bugsy dislikes the bum, but knows from experience he can do business with the man. "Mr. Mount, your organization is doing well, I take it?" Bugsy is always on best behavior when surrounded by so many suits.

"Reasonably well, Mr. Siegel, I can't complain. Usual ups and downs."

Bugsy nods in appreciation. Mount wouldn't last a day on the street. They both know it. Bugsy and Mount have a mutual interest in maintaining status quo. It's a well oiled apple cart.

"Exactly, Mr. Mount? My Union and the studios are in agreement? It's in all of our best interests there be no interruption in the production cycle? Am I correct here, Mr. Mount?"

"Absolutely, Mr. Siegel."

"Excellent? So, Mr. Mount, are you still satisfied taking in more than a thousand times per year what the average member of my Union makes a year? It is about a thousand times, isn't it, Mr. Mount? I wouldn't want you to want, now would I, Mr. Mount?"

Mount does not reply.

Bugsy continues. "Yeah, I thought you'd be satisfied? Well, most of you know I'm not originally from around here? Right?" General nods around the table. "Now where I come from, we have our share of problems too? Nothing as complicated as the negotiations now at hand, but tricky enough to keep guys like me busy? Right?"

Nods all around.

"Now can I assume all of us in this room are living a pretty comfortable life? Right?" More nods. "And we can agree that what often times gets in the way of business being run in a businesslike fashion is somebody gets a little greedy and they stop behaving in a reasonable manner?

"Now what are we supposed to do with somebody who is out of line with their greed and refuses to do business in a businesslike manner?" There is no response from those at the table.

"I find it hard to believe anyone in this room wants to see the poor working men and women of my Union work for even less money than the handouts they're getting under the present contract? With all the money coming to the people sitting in this room, I don't see why my guys aren't paid enough to eat? Does anyone here have a problem with that?" At this point, Bugsy allows himself to show displeasure. Not much, just enough to let it be known. He wants to see these men slightly frightened.

"None at all." is the general response.

"Are you all comfortable with your lives the way they are now? Do any of us want to see our way of life drastically altered?" Bugsy is on a roll. He sees the sweat begin to bead on the faces of his audience. Bugsy is the tough teacher and these are reluctant students.

"Gentlemen, we have a good thing going here? Now it looks to me like some or you are trying to queer the deal by getting greedy? I'm not asking much for my people, am I? I mean we all have to eat, don't we?" Bugsy presents his case in as reasonable a way as possible. The studio heads have to see the logic of his argument.

Mount speaks again. "Mr. Siegel, allow me to assure you, everyone sitting at this table is willing to sign the new contract immediately. Right now. Today. We, here, have no problems with the terms of the contract. What's causing the delay are the bankers in New York. They won't extend our existing lines of credit any further if we sign. They maintain it's a bad precedent and they're drawing the line. Mr. Siegel, New York is blocking us. There's really nothing we can do about it."

Same old crap. Pass the blame off on someone else. These guys wouldn't know how to take responsibility if their lives depended on it. A warm, red, wet mist appears before Bugsy's eyes. For him, the room becomes completely silent. What little motion there is slows to nothing. Two minutes pass as Bugsy stands in front of the table and does nothing. As the mist clears Bugsy sees everything in the room in minute detail. Every pressed lapel. Every chin hair missed by this morning's razor. He hears air escaping from the lungs of individual executives. Bugsy's mind records so much detailed information, that if one motion within the room feels out of place, it's possible Bugsy might explode into action.

Around the table, the executives of Hollywood sense the change. They've watched faces on the screen for decades and Ben Siegel's face has become a roadmap for disaster. All they hope for now is the disaster won't involve them.

"You know, Mr. Mount," Bugsy momentarily returns from his altered state to a place where action can be replaced by discussion of action. "I thought as much? It didn't figure you guys would want to screw up the good thing we have going here?" Heads nod around the table. "Let's say we take a break and meet back here in a half hour? O.K.? Good?" Ben "Bugsy" Siegel calls the meeting to a temporary halt.

Exiting the room, Bugsy walks over to the Union leader. "Marty, give Meyer a call, will you. Tell him he should keep the appointment. O.K.. Good."

In an outer office located on the seventy-eighth floor of a Manhattan skyscraper, two men dressed in conservative business suits approach a secretary sitting at her desk.

The shorter of the two men speaks, "We'd like to see Mr. Lucien."

Looking the visitors over, the secretary does not like what she sees. The men are dressed properly but their rough faces don't go with the quality of their suits. "I'm sorry but Mr. Lucien is not available at the moment. Would you care to make an appointment?"

The taller of the two steps behind the desk and puts one hand over the woman's mouth while his other arms wraps around her mid-section, lifting her out of the chair and into the air.

Realizing she is at a complete disadvantage, the woman does not struggle.

Opening the door between the outer and inner offices, the

shorter of the two men sees Lucien sitting at his desk in front of a wide window overlooking a neighborhood park . Moving with a speed inappropriate to an office environment, the smaller man is immediately behind the startled Lucien. Grabbing the moderately overweight business leader from his chair, the smaller man carries the startled financier to the window and with a display of surprising strength, grabs Lucien's left leg, raises the now parallel-to-the-floor business man to chest height, and tosses him through the glass window.

It takes close to four seconds before Lucien's body lands on the sidewalk alongside the building.

As the two men leave the office, the taller man plops the shocked secretary back in her chair.

"We were never here." The little man tosses an envelope onto the secretary's desk. Opening it, she sees an inch thick assortment of hundred dollar bills. As the two men leave the office and head towards the elevator, the secretary sticks the envelope into her purse and follows them out the door but turns in the opposite direction, towards the powder room down the hall. The secretary saw nothing and was not in the office at the time Mr. Lucien committed suicide. Or so the official report will read.

Recalling the meeting to order, Bugsy sees on the faces surrounding him that these Hollywood executives were in communication with New York during the break.

The meeting rapidly comes to a close. Minor concessions are made on behalf of both the Studios and the Union, and word is sent to the negotiators to wrap it all up. Bugsy shakes hands with these would be wage slavers and heads back to his other job.

Back on the set the company is still filming the same set-up. Bugsy hasn't missed a thing. He reports back to the Director's assistant. Bugsy finds his place amid the background players.

"Mr. Siegel, the Director would like a word with you."

The rest of his fellow Union members are impressed. Though most of them already know who Bugsy is, being summoned by the Director is an honor they can only envy.

"Mr. Siegel, I'd like you to read these lines at the end of the scene."

Bugsy knows what this is all about. The Director's has been given an order by the suits at the Studio to be nice to Mr. Siegel. He knows his lines will most certainly end up on the cutting room floor. But Bugsy still enjoys the process of making movies and when he's on the set, he'll go
along with just about anything.

"Quiet, please. Rolling."

Bugsy's lines aren't until the very end of the scene. Until then he mingles with the other extras and watches as the principal players perform their roles. Bugsy checks his costume making sure everything is in its proper place. For the first time, he wonders if his period wardrobe had any influence on the contract discussions just concluded.

Now that crazy Australian Flynn kisses the girl.

Now the King waves towards the people.

Now Bugsy steps forward and delivers his line. It's not often the village blacksmith in one of these movies gets to speak.

"Long live Richard the Lionhearted? Long live Robin Hood?"

As Bugsy expects, his lines land on the cutting room floor. But he still gets full pay and residuals. That's what the Union contract stipulates.

GRAY FLANNEL KIMONO

Early morning in the park. Very early. An ascending sun engages the morning mist. A couple strolls arm in arm along the pathway. Two merlins cut figures in the sky. Sounds of a neighborhood awakening encroach upon the park's tranquility. A yellow sedan sedately cruises an adjoining street. One choice thud is heard as a young woman hurls this morning's paper from the vehicle's passenger window, landing gently on the front steps of another suburban home. Laughter is heard as trash cans being unloaded into an inordinately pummeled truck collide. Women and men in sweat suits approach this compact park from all points of the compass.

They form two lines. A gray haired man stands alone before his assembly. He stares into the eyes of the five running togged people in each file. He stretches his arms toward the merlins, who respond by soaring west, away from the park. The sun has fully risen. The eleven begin their work.

"Breathe!" He speaks, releasing his limbs from the sky, dropping them nearer to earth. Two columns respond, mirroring his exact movement.

"Breathe!" The teacher assumes a squatting position, but he does not rest. His legs stay flexed but taut. His hands reach forward, fingers thrust ahead, arched, isolated. The ten follow his lead.

Moving in harmony, they straighten their legs, stretch their spines, and extend fingers farther and farther from their bodies. Elongating their reach, they extend the limits of the unified scope, past the unit's initial expectations.

"Breathe!" The instructor commands. Synchronously, the collective grip veers left then right, shadowing their instructor's motions. Hardening arms define the air, languidly sketching figure eights. Torsos and hips emulate the movement. The session continues for fifteen unified minutes.

"Breathe!" The master, motionless, dictates. His students halt, limbs thrust high above their bodies.

"Stay!" And the maestro lowers his hands, turning his back to the novices.

They remain stationary, hands stretched above frames. The maestro strides away, crossing the lea. They watch in extended agony as he enters his van and departs.

When the van disappears from view, the disciples diminish tension within their individual bodies. A man falls to the ground. A few in the group keep their arms outstretched, only imperceptibly bringing disciplined extremities from the air. Leigh briskly drops her limbs to her sides, bends forward, and potently inhales three times.

In their kitchen Miles prepares breakfast. Taking a chef's knife in his right hand, he slides two peeled bananas to the center of a cutting board, precisely segmenting them into uniform disks. He reaches above his head. Opening the cupboard, Miles removes two medium-sized crockery bowls, along with a clear glass canister containing bran cereal. He moves the three objects onto a corner table set for breakfast, empties the canister into the bowls, double checks a container of milk, rearranges some spoons, then moves a vase of flowers a few inches from its original location. Smiling at the arrangement, he migrates towards the refrigerator to collect some orange juice.

Leigh enters the kitchen through the screen door. Her face afire from the exertion of her morning run. Miles closes the refrigerator door and puts the orange juice carton on the counter. He turns to his wife, "Hungry?"

"Give me a minute. I'll be right with you." Leigh smiles at Miles who adjusts his worn robe. She continues her way through the kitchen into the bathroom.

Turning on the shower, Leigh is half out of her sweats. Miles retrieves juice glasses from the cabinet above his head. He wanders to the table while listening to the streaming shower. He pours juice into the glasses and starts back to the refrigerator. On the way, he pauses to scratch his still unshaven chin. Closing the refrigerator door, he hears the water stop. He moves to the cutting board to slide banana fragments onto a plate. Miles moves back to the table. Leigh, blotting her short hair with a towel, joins him.

Leigh appraises her breakfast, "Lovely.", smiles momentarily, then opens a cabinet door on her left. She clicks on the television stock market report, scrutinizing the screen for thirty seconds, then turns full attention to her meal.

"Sounds like the markets aren't performing well today." Miles wipes his mouth while delivering his commentary. "Think you'll be late getting back tonight?"

Leigh finishes chewing then responds. "Not to worry. The firm's anticipating possible retrograde activity, perhaps for the entire quarter. Phyllis' group will handle any swings in the peripheral markets. All we have on the docket remotely interesting is the Yokimora Proposal."

They finish their cereal. Miles carries spent bowls, glasses, and silverware to the sink.

Leigh checks the wall clock. "I'm not going to be late." She stands, relinquishing the kitchen. Removing her terry cloth robe, she enters the bedroom.

Miles rinses the final dishes, places them in the machine, and snaps it on. As the dishwasher begins its program, Miles runs more water from the tap and cranks up the garbage disposal. The machine grinds until Miles flips the wall switch.

On her car radio, Leigh tunes in trance music. She cruises the middle lane of a three lane highway amid the rush hour mob of soon to be late employees. A speeding maroon Jaguar convertible becomes visible in Leigh's rear view mirror. It soars up to her car's bumper, dominating the mirror's glass. Leigh fails to notice, listening to her stereo while performing wrist exercises against the steering wheel.

The Jag pulls into the far left lane. The driver glares at Leigh.

She remains oblivious to him. He edges the Jag near the bumper of the car ahead of him. He abruptly cuts right, missing the front left end of Leigh's car by millimeters. Leigh slowly moves her head back and forth, exercising her fingers during the Jag's stunts. She does not react to the Jag's abrupt maneuver. The Jag pulls into another lane. Leigh lowers the volume of her radio.

Miles sits at the living room coffee table fiddling with an open briefcase perched in front of him. He takes his hands from the briefcase, removes his glasses, then rubs the bridge of his nose. He straightens his tie, staring at the ceiling, then randomly scans the room. He removes a ballpoint pen from his vest pocket and begins taking notes on a yellow legal pad alongside the briefcase.

Again he leans forward. Placing his hands inside the brief case, Miles types a few characters on the computer contained within. He glances at the yellow sheet reading the words, "collaborative takeover". Striking more keys, the screen goes blank. Miles moves to his right and unplugs the cable connecting the briefcase and wall. He closes the case, locks it, grabs his suit jacket, puts it on, picks up the case, then deciding not to take the legal pad with him, Miles leaves his home.

A conservatively dressed woman steps through an office door. "They're ready for you now." She addresses the rear of a wool upholstered, high back, executive chair.

As the chair spins forward to the woman, Leigh snatches a small portfolio case from the floor beside her desk. "It's about time. Fay, have the prospectuses been distributed?"

"It's out there. Whether or not they comprehend it or not, who knows? It'd serve them right if they've as much trouble figuring it out as I did when I read the directions to set up my stereo system."

Leigh is not amused. "Not the point, Fay. We're cutting a deal today. That's all we can allow ourselves on our consciousnesses. Your problems with convoluted technospeak have nothing to do with it. I'd appreciate if you'd keep that thought in the front of your mind during the meeting." Leigh snatches papers from Fay Wreath's hand. "You stay close, Fay. I'll show you how it's done." Leigh exits the office as her aide follows.

Partially encircling an elliptical, blonde mahogany conference table, four business suited people raise their eyes when Leigh Adams and Fay Wreath enter the room. Taking two unoccupied seats, Adams and Wreath turn their attention to the chairwoman, Kendall Lane, who begins the meeting.

"Since I'm sure we all know who we all are, I'll bypass formal introductions. Now that our vice-president for corporate acquisitions, Leigh Adams, and her assistant, Fay Wreath, have arrived, we can tend to the business at hand. Is there anything anyone would like to say before we begin?"

Gazing down the table, the chairwoman nods in the direction of an elderly man, Foster Fog, who toys with a ring on his small finger. Fog starts to speak.

"Ms. Lane, as we are all well aware, my firm arrives at this table with a good deal of reluctance. Perhaps apprehension would be a better word. Our organization has been in business for quite some time. We scrutinize, with a generous deal of skepticism, any firm that speaks of superior methods to be used within a territory where we've been the dominant force for many years. We are, however, quite willing to listen to any original concepts you might propose."

Saying this, the elderly gentleman turns to his associates on his left and right. "And if the three of you have any questions, I'm sure my companions can assist you." Nodding to his confederates, he makes eye contact with the three women from the Enigma Group. Foster Fog then promptly falls asleep.

"As our esteemed chairman has made clear," this is Hiram Ambler, the president of the firm speaking. He stands to the right of the napper. "For decades our firm has possessed exclusive marketing licenses over a vast, and not speaking pompously, quite lucrative market share.

"It is not now our intention, nor do we make any pretense to perceive in the imminent future, any need to respond to your not quite generous tender offer. But, as has been stated, we are willing listeners to any reasonable proposals which may be of mutual benefit to all concerned parties." With this the president of Ectoterra sits. His conscious partner, Richard Chaise, legal counsel, appears unable to withhold a sense of alarm, listening to his co-worker's words. As Ambler sits, Richard Chaise clears his throat. Kendall Lane nods in his direction.

"My name is Richard Chaise, corporate counsel for Ectoterra. According to my brief, issued at the last meeting of our Board of Directors, I am presently empowered to offer the Enigma Group a number of alternatives which will make this merger mutually attractive.

"I have been empowered by our Yokimora division to offer Enigma sole proprietary rights within..."

"Am I correct in assuming you speak for Ectoterra as the prime negotiator?" Leigh Adams now leans forward in her chair, her face inches from that of Ectoterra's legal counsel. Her voice combines both generosity and rage.

"Ms. Adams, my Board of Directors has dealt with numerous hostile takeover attempts in the past. They feel quite secure in their ability to thwart any threat in the future. The Board met one week ago. Since leaving that meeting, Mr. Fog, Mr. Ambler, and myself have been your most grateful guests. I assure you, my opinion of your operation has altered immensely. However, I am vested with limited authority. I can only speak for myself in regards to anything other than the Board's initial offer." Richard Chaise leans back in his chair. He is perspiring and alarmed.

Hiram Ambler espies his counsel with consummate contempt. "I can assure Enigma that Mr. Chaise speaks only for himself. Ectoterra has yet to decide upon the corporate position to be assumed regarding your enterprise. Other than that, we are here to simply observe and report."

Which doesn't sit entirely well with either Leigh Adams or, especially, Fay Wreath, who at this moment is sinking her teeth into a yellow legal sized pad in a laudable effort to keep from screaming. As her anger subsides, she notices Richard Chaise.

"Mr. Ambler, we're puzzling if you are absolutely cognizant of how tenuous your present position is?" Leigh Adams addresses this corporate prince with less than the respect to which he has grown accustomed. "Ectoterra has expanded considerably within the last five decades. Growth like this can hardly be ignored. Or, at the very least, ignored with singular jeopardy. We've not come to this table to discuss your Yokimora division. We've not come to this table to discuss a merger with Ectoterra. We've come to this table to resolve what, if any, positions the former employees of Ectoterra will have within the expanded structure of the Enigma Group."

Leigh Adams leans back in her chair. Leafing through a prospectus, she completes her overview. "Mr. Ambler, whether you have been advised of it or not, since nine o'clock this morning, Eastern Standard Time, the firm of Ectoterra...." But she does not continue since Ambler is now shaking the shoulders of a drowsing Foster Fog. The senior member of the firm does not respond in the way Hiram Ambler desires. Instead of activating the master businessman within himself, Foster Fog begins humming a tune from a long forgotten Broadway show. He smiles at some hidden thought, apparently within a deep sleep.

Fay Wreath now stands directly behind Richard Chaise. With left hand clutching her legal pad and notes, she places the right on the legal counsel's shoulder. "Are you taken?"

Which is not exactly what Richard Chaise expects to hear. He swivels in his seat, confronting the woman standing above him. "Is this in the prospectus?"

Fay smiles. She whispers in the lawyer's ear while Hiram Ambler continues his attempts to rouse the Chairman of the Board. "Sir, if you'll excuse me, sir. We're having a rather critical meeting here, sir. Sir? Would you be so kind to acknowledge my request. Sir?"

None of which seems to phase Kendall Lane in the least. She's retrieved her knitting and stitches some sort of scarf. Leigh Adams remains seated, perusing the contents of her portfolio case. With great concentration she extracts and begins reading a copy of "Archaeology Today".

"Is this the way your firm usually conducts its business?" It's Ambler again, who at this point has given up any attempt to stir Fog, who has proceeded from humming Broadway tunes to conducting an illusory orchestra which plays, as far as anyone can tell from the unpracticed gestures of his hands and arms, something akin to Vivaldi.

"We do the best we can, given the framework of established business procedures." Leigh does not glance away from her magazine.

"Mr. Ambler, if you'll excuse us a few minutes, Ms. Wreath and I would like to discuss some of the ancillary positions, aspects, of the negotiations." Richard Chaise is already following Fay who holds the conference door ajar.

"Mr. Chaise, since our Chairman appears incapacitated at the moment, I do believe this meeting is adjourned. Go right ahead." Ambler delivers his approval with the expression of a man who has had discussions with executive assistants, concerning ancillary positions, a few times himself.

"Thank you, sir." Richard Chaise tracks Fay Wreath's trail from the conference room.

"Now, Mr. Ambler," Leigh Adams closes the pages of her magazine and tosses it on the table. "What exactly is the Yokimora Proposal? We don't have a great deal of time for any nonsense."

Richard Chaise sits on a couch in Fay Wreath's office, reading from a yellow legal pad on the low table in front of him. "You have all of the pertinent points on Yokimora fairly well summarized. How did you get this information?"

"It's not that hard. The Enigma Group considered the existing technology, your firm's track record, then extrapolated to the most degenerate degree we dared imagine. How'd you think you'd get away with it?" Fay Wreath squats in front of the low table, her long skirt covering her ankles.

"I didn't think it was the most exalted of ideas, but, you don't understand, the firm can do it. If it can be done, it's going to be done. Do you understand that? It's the basis of all technological innovation."

Fay moves now. She lifts herself from the floor to sit on the couch next to Richard. "You know it's sick but you want to continue. Even with my being next to you, you want to maintain the Yokimora Proposal."

"Can't you appreciate its elegance? I'm not saying I agree with it, but it's possible. One single cell from the proper donor. The factory could be here in the States." Richard is obviously fascinated by the concept. "Infinite replication."

"Infinite replication of what?" Fay is again on her feet. "Infinite replication of what? Don't give me infinite replication of anything human." Now Richard Chaise is on his feet himself. "What would anyone with a job like yours know about anything like this. Some of the world's top biologists and geneticists worked on this project. We can create life anywhere."

"You have no idea what life is. Life isn't cells that multiply in a void. There's no safety." Fay turns from Richard and faces the wall.

Chaise continues. "The idea is to maintain life. There's no

other way to avoid the catastrophe. None of us is going to live forever. But there are those who will pay. They'll pay a great deal to know they will, somehow, exist. Forever."

"You send cells, suspended in nothing, into space, to avoid conditions of your own conception? You understand what you're doing?" Fay feels as if she's speaking into the void herself.

The lawyers mind is again preoccupied with the elegance of the Yokimora Proposal. "Thousands of years from now, somewhere in the universe, a ship descends upon a planet deemed hospitable to human life. It remains semi-dormant taking readings of atmosphere and environment. Then, at the optimum moment, the craft opens itself to a new world. Some days later, new cells take form. In a few weeks, after the proper amount of cocooning, a new man emerges, fully educated by the most superb teaching machines ever designed. Later, others follow. But the first, the first is the honor. Can you imagine how they'll pay to be the first new man, the last man alive." The counsel sprawls himself on the couch as he engages in his own form of mental ecstasy.

Fay kneels near the edge of the couch. "All of the resources of Ectoterra are behind the Yokimora Proposal. Everything your firm's accumulated is at the disposal of this plan. You understand what that means?"

Richard Chaise has the glow of a man with a vision. "One man. For a hell of a lot of cash, one man will have it. I'll be there. They won't know which. I'll be close. I can be the man. Let them pay for the illusion.

"I know the law. I know who'll make the decision. I know them all, inside out. They'll do what I want. None of them is clean.

I'll make it out someway. They think it will be one of them, but when the smoke clears, it'll be me." The legal counsel now makes an offer out of blind affection. "Work with me. We can take them all."

Fay sits beside Richard. "Where did you come up with these recommendations? We knew this would be part of the proposal. It's elegant, but it's no deal. Ectoterra exists so it will be utilized. But not with your way. We're tired of it. The market problems you can't resolve in your own minds, you try to escape." Fay Wreath strokes Richard Chaise's cheek with her hand. "Don't you understand, it will destroy not only your firm, but ours. We don't want either circumstance to occur. There are other ways of conducting business." Again the fear seen within the lawyer's eyes during the conference room meeting spreads across his face. He wavers. "There can't be?"

Fay Wreath gleams compassionately at poor Richard. "We'll have to find another way. Won't we?" She kisses him on the lips.

Kendall Lane still knits what appears to be a scarf. She speaks. "Sixty percent seems eminently fair to me." Foster Fog, back from his musical comedy career, agrees. "Sixty percent, ninety percent, a hundred and ten percent. Whatever you think's correct is O.K. in my book." Saying this he sits back in his chair and smiles.

On hearing the door to the conference room open, Hiram Ambler turns from the chairwoman to see Fay Wreath enter, followed by Richard Chaise. Both seem quite pleased with themselves. Ambler is not amused. "Chaise, they're stripping us down to our skivvies here. Is any of this legal?"

As the couple return to their seats, Leigh Adams looks up from her magazine. She addresses the chair. "I believe control of seventy percent of Ectoterra's voting stock would be more beneficial to our shareholders, madam."

Which almost brings Hiram Ambler to his feet but a small look from Lane sits him down again. He addresses Chaise, "I suppose you knew about Ectoterra's stock before you came in this morning?"

"Not really, Mr. Ambler, though I tell you, I couldn't imagine any other reason for our being here. What happened to the stock?"

Leigh Adams glances up from her magazine, and looking towards Richard Chaise, for the second time today, she smiles.

Leigh lowers the volume of a waltz playing on her car stereo. A car horn has her look to the right lane where a driver emphatically urges the car in front of him to speed up. Continuing to cruise, she passes a maroon Jaguar on her right. The driver is nervously scrutinizing the road in all directions as he crawls along the highway, fifteen miles per hour under the speed limit.

Miles, dressed in old clothes, uproots weeds in the front garden. Leigh pulls into the driveway. From the car she calls to her husband. "Dinner ready?"

Miles looks up from his toil, sweat pouring from his brow, "Whenever you're ready, only have to pop it in the oven."

Leigh smiles again, "Lovely." She enters their home. Miles continues weeding. Leigh, now similarly dressed in old clothes, kneels beside him, helping complete the gardening. They work together a few moments then Miles leans to his wife and kisses her on the cheek. "How are things with Yokimora?"

Another morning in the park. The risen sun hides behind a

bank of clouds. Ten people perform exercises, opposing themselves within the circle. Two merlins soar overhead. A sedan sedately cruises an adjoining street. A newspaper is delivered. Laughter is heard.

NO COLD HAM AND EGGS

Gloria's on the bus. She strokes her hair and touches the collar of her blouse. She glances at others riding this off-hours afternoon transport.

Across the aisle Gloria spots an ancient woman rummaging through a shopping bag. For a moment Gloria studies her. She discovers the person within the worn clothing. She's inspired by the strength of the woman's spine. Gloria notices the older woman adjust her faded coat. She watches her watching over a pair of young girls on their way home from grammar school. She examines the matriarch as the matriarch examines the two emerging women sing to one another. An elderly man naps, resting his head on the woman's shoulder.

A chime is heard. The bus pulls to the curb. Gloria hefts her shoulder bag, aligns her skirt and strides to the front of the bus. The two girls smile in Gloria's direction. The dowager raises her eyes, tilting her head forward. Gloria navigates the bus's steps.

Inside the restaurant a woman Gloria's age orders tea. The man accompanying the tea drinker smokes a cigarette. He orders whiskey. Gloria turns her back to her customers. She steps to the service bar.

"We were wondering when you'd get here." Sylvia's shift began hours ago. Her blouse carries a hundred meals' stains. Her once permanent curls sag across her forehead. What was an open smile now scarcely raises the corners of her mouth.

"There was a problem on the bus." Gloria gives a bartender her order. She prepares tea.

"Are you all right?" Sylvia starts back to the dining room then stops to listen some more. Sylvia is concerned.

"There was a problem with two passengers on the bus. The driver had to pull over then we had to wait a long time for a replacement bus and driver. I'm O.K."

"Good. 'Cause my shift ends in another ten minutes." Sylvia heads back to her tables. Gloria brews someone else's drink.

Gloria's soiled blouse now displays her shift's eight hours. Her hair droops into her eyes. Gloria leans on the bar. Again she prepares tea for another woman. The bartender positions a glass on her tray. Gloria wanders into the dining room.

The tables are mostly vacant. There are two occupied booths in her section. Gloria moves to a seated couple to deliver their order. She watches the man place his hand over his companion's. The woman sheds tears. He speaks in tones most indulgent.

Gloria pauses then dispenses the drinks. The man looks up. He removes his hand. The woman, tears on her cheeks, raises her head. The two women exchange glances. "Is there anything else I can get you?"

The woman stares quizzically. The man smiles at Gloria. The woman sees the man smile. The woman speaks to her escort when she addresses Gloria. "You can bring us our check."

Late in the evening Gloria prepares for bed. She takes the telephone into her hand, wonders who to call, places it back on the hook. From the window of her undersized room she peers down three stories into the street. Cars and cabs pass with regularity, the flow orchestrated by the corner traffic light. Gloria shivers, turns off the lamp, and goes to bed.

In the morning she walks a building corridor. People dressed for the bureaucratic life pass her by. She searches for an office number scribbled on an index card. Wandering the hallway, Gloria becomes more confused. People swarm about, uttering syllables from a language only vaguely related to her life. She rests on a bench a few moments. She compares the clothes worn by the passing women with her own. A vagrant stops, parks beside her and smiles. Gloria looks at him briefly, stands, then leaves. She's less startled than the vagrant hoped she'd be. Gloria continues down the hall.

A woman behind a desk motions Gloria to sit. The woman picks up a phone, listens, and speaks four words. "He'll see you now." She points to a door. Gloria rises from the barely dented chair. She walks to the door marked "Assistant District Investigator". She knocks. "No, honey, you go right on in." She looks at the receptionist. Opening the door, Gloria walks through.

"Sit down, Miss Williams, I'll be with you in a minute." Gloria takes another seat. She waits. The man speaks into the telephone.

A woman sits to the side of the man's desk. She slightly smiles at Gloria.

"Yes, sir, she came in this minute. Right. I certainly will do that, sir. No, thank you, sir. Right. On your desk within the hour. Thank you, sir. Goodbye." He replaces the handset while addressing the other woman.

"Debbie, entertain Miss Williams for a few minutes while I go down the hall. Miss Williams, this is Debbie. She'll be here while I'm gone." He smiles. "I'll be right back." He opens the door, closing it behind himself.

The two women exchange questioning stares.

Gloria adjusts to her seat while scanning the office. There's the desk where the man was sitting until a few seconds ago. The walls are covered with framed certificates and photographs. Everything in the room seems new. There are a number of chrome accents including a desk light and a large planter next to the desk, across from Debbie. The office shows great attention has been paid to cleanliness and function.

"Miss Williams, Mr. Plover will be right back. Is there anything I can get for you?" Debbie stares at Gloria daring a request. Gloria again shifts in her seat. She stares at the floor. "No thank you, miss. I'll be fine here."

"If that's the way you like it." At which point Debbie ends all semblance of civility. She begins studying the notebook in her hands. After a moment she turns her back to Gloria.

Gloria stares at her own hands. She stares at the floor. Debbie puts her steno book on the desk. She lights a cigarette.

Gloria clears her throat. Debbie turns. The two women again

exchange looks. Gloria takes out a handkerchief to wipe her nose. Debbie continues smoking.

Time passes.

Gloria lifts her head. Plover enters the office. He sits behind his desk. Debbie crushes out her cigarette. She takes up her steno pad.

Plover touches his upper lip with a pencil top eraser. He leans back in his chair. Amiably he inquires, "Miss Williams, we heard it from other people but we'd like to hear it from you. What exactly happened on the bus yesterday ?"

There are nights when Gloria stumbles home late in the evening with barely enough strength to undress before falling into bed. There are mornings when it takes all her strength lacing work shoes over swollen feet. There are times when Gloria would gladly stick a piece of flatware into some customer's neck if anyone gave her a nickel to do it. Gloria is not thrilled with her job, not thrilled with her life, in general, no longer thrilled about anything. Now she has to tell what happened yesterday on the bus while an unrepentant smoker takes notes. Gloria is not thrilled about this either.

"You want me to tell you about the bus?"

Plover rocks peacefully in his chair. He nods. The pencil which has been scratching his upper lip now scratches the back of his ear. Debbie clears her throat, looks at her steno book, straightens her back, awaiting the onslaught. Gloria begins.

"Well, like you said, you may have heard some of this from the others on the bus. I don't want to bore you with anything you've already heard, but like you said, you've heard some of this already from some of the other people but now you'd like to hear it from me. All right.

"Some mornings, you know how hard it is to get out of bed? It's not that I'm lazy or anything like that, it's only some mornings it's hard to see why anyone should have to leave their place and go someplace else so somebody else can have a good time and another person can make money from what they're working at doing. Everybody knows what it feels like and don't get the idea I'm complaining or anything, it's only some mornings, especially after I've worked hard the whole day before, it's hard getting moving in the morning so's you can get back to starting the whole thing over again."

Plover nods.

"I see you know what I mean. Yesterday was like that a whole lot. I'd worked real late, again, again, and I would of given myself a whole day's tips not to have to have to get out of bed, but I didn't have the money to pay myself, so I didn't, and I got up.

"The bus is usually a little late. That doesn't bother me since I always remember to take its being late into account, so I leave a little early, so I get to work on time. I was the only one at the stop, it's sort of off hours for them when I take the bus, and the driver pulls over nice as can be. Everything is fine.

"I know as soon as I get on something's wrong. The driver doesn't say hello like usual and he takes the fare like he's thinking about something else. Usually he gives me a big hello and it's a nice way to start the day. I've been taking his bus for three years now. I like him saying hello every day.

"I take my usual seat, the one right behind the driver, and look around to see if there's anyone I know riding today. There are only nine or ten people on the bus and I haven't seen any of them before, so I start looking out the window.

"I hear them a long time before I actually turn around to look at them. May I have a drink of water?"

Debbie, the stenographer, puts down her book, walks to the water cooler, and fetches Gloria some water. It's been a long time since anyone waited on Gloria. Unfortunately, the stenographer becomes aware the waitress enjoys being served. Debbie returns to her seat in silence.

Plover nods. Gloria sips her drink.

"At first I think they're only having a little argument. Something between a girlfriend and a boyfriend like. They aren't making much noise, but they're moving around a whole lot. They're in the middle of the bus and the other passengers want to ignore them and get off quick as they can. Everybody seems to be fidgeting around a lot back there.

"I'm trying to listen real hard to hear what they're saying to each other.

"The woman jumps out from where she's sitting and starts yelling at the man. Right when she's doing this the driver changes gears so I can't hear what she's yelling. When the bus changes gears it sort of moves forward in a jerky way, and the woman is knocked off balance and she has to grab on to the rail behind her so she won't fall down. The man watches her, doesn't move to help out at all.

"This really gets her mad. I don't know if the two of them are drunk, on drugs, or what. She screams at him, `You fool. Get off your butt and help me!' He sits there, smiles, and doesn't even raise his little finger. All he says is, `You wanted to go. What's your problem now?' Only he says it real sarcastic like, not like I'm saying it at all. This gets her even madder.

"Then she really gets angry and starts cursing him up and down. Now everybody on the bus is looking at them and I look in the rear view mirror and the driver is looking at them too. They're acting real strange.

"I'm looking at the driver to see if he's going to do anything about those two when I hear the scream. I turn around real fast and it's not the woman in the aisle who's screaming, but an older woman who's sitting only a few feet behind me across the aisle, who's doing the screaming. I see her look to the back of the bus and she's staring at the woman standing all alone.

"The woman in the aisle is holding something. I can't see what it is because she's leaning over where the man is sitting. The other woman stops screaming and is moving up the aisle past me to the front. Everyone else on the bus is staring and not really moving. I don't know what's going on and I'm a little scared.

"The woman is leaning in front of the man and I can't see him for a second or two. I turn around to the front because the bus has started to sway back and forth. The elderly woman is shaking the bus driver trying to get him to pull to the side of the road. The driver is pushing her away and telling her he's pulling over and to sit down. When I turn back to the couple the woman is sitting next to the man again. The man's head is sagging on his chest and the woman is smiling. I can't see the man's face 'cause it's leaning forward so far.

"The driver pulls the bus to the curb and stops. We all sort of bounce forward. I turn real quick and look at the driver and when I turn back again, the man's head is no longer on his chest, it's fallen back and seems to be balancing on the top of his seat. The most spookiest thing I've ever seen."

Gloria pauses a moment. She sips her water. "He may be dead. I can't tell. I hope not."

"Take your time, Miss Williams, I know this can't be very easy for you."

"It's not like I've never seen somebody hurt before. It's that he sort of sits there like he's waiting for something. He has this strange expression on his face, like everything is going to be all right so long as everyone stays quiet and relaxed.

"The woman is standing in the aisle again. She's smiling or something, it's not like anything I've seen lately."

"Would you like some more water?"

"No. But thanks all the same. He's sitting in that same spot with his head jangling on the back of his seat like he's some sort of puppet. There isn't a mark on him I can see.

"The driver comes down and checks the man's pulse. I remember him saying, `What you done to this guy, lady?'

"She's standing there with that odd smile of hers and doesn't say a word. She doesn't move but she's also sort of swaying in the aisle. Not like a dance or anything like that but like she's in a trance or something.

"The driver doesn't seem to know what to do. Most of the other passengers have gotten off the bus already. I think I remember it's about this time I guess there must be a police car or an ambulance next to the bus, because I'm watching red lights swirl on the woman's face. It must've been a red police light but I remember other colors too.

"This is real difficult for me to explain but I'll give it a try. By now there isn't a soul on the bus, except me and the driver, and the woman and the man. I'm trying to describe her face. There are lights surrounding her eyes that make her look like she's at an amusement park, or a rock concert. She's swaying in the aisle while the colors bounce all over her body. She's swaying, and smiling, and all those weird lights are dancing on her face.

"'I'm out of here.' That's what the driver says. And he runs right past me. He leaves me alone with an unconscious man and a woman who doesn't look human anymore."

"What did she appear to be?" Plover now gnaws his pencil.

"She's like an angel. Or a devil. Or both. I don't know. I'm frightened but I can't move. Then she starts coming towards me. I can't move. She opens her mouth like she wants to say something.

"I start moving closer to her. My legs are moving by themselves. We're only a few inches from one another. She has her face so its only an inch from mine."

Gloria stops speaking. She sips water. She looks at the man behind the desk. Plover stares at Gloria with his mouth slightly open. Debbie stops taking notes to scrutinize Gloria's eyes.

"Her face is so close to mine. Her eyes are wide open. She puts her lips next to my ear and whispers, 'Everything's all right.' And then she falls into my arms.

"That's when the paramedics and the police come. They take

my name, ask me some questions, and I have to wait over an hour for another bus to take me to work."

Gloria, bowing her head, ends her narrative. She feels the blood coursing through her veins. Plover and Debbie observe Gloria in silence.

Plover at last slants his body forward on the desk. His elbows press down on the blotter. Two fists support his chin. "An exceptionally interesting story, Miss Williams, but you understand, there's never a good reason for being late to work."

And on the television screen we see the Waitress reacting to the Assistant District Investigator's comment. Her face reflects astonishment on hearing the Investigator's words.

Viewing this instructional film is a group of twelve employees from the Enigma Restaurants chain. The instructor stands and turns off the video player. One of the dozen people sitting around the oval table raises her hand.

"Are we going to be paid for the time we've been here, or are we watching all this stuff for free?"

A few others nod their heads in agreement while a young waitress sitting near the back of the room stares at the instructor with obvious contempt.

HOLY AGNES

I like this place. There are nice people here. Sometimes we sing. Now and then the young girl comes to visit me. She brings her little kitty. The kitty isn't Patches. Patches was black and white. The little girl's kitty is brown and white. I can't remember the girl's name. Patches went out at night and never came back. I like the young girl and her kitty. But her kitty isn't Patches.

"Agnes, dinner."

That's the waitress I don't like. No, I like her but she doesn't like me.

"Dinner, Agnes. Come on. You can watch your programs later."

All the meals are nice. I don't have to cook anymore. And the food is free. I can eat all I want and sometimes I sneak snacks back to my room. I think they know I take food but the waitresses don't mind.

"Good girl, Agnes. Dinner's tasty tonight, isn't it?"

I used to cook. Pot roast. I can smell the cooking now. Time for dinner. Call Al and our boy to the table. Sunday dinner after Church. Cooking for my two handsome men.

The boy. All the young boys. I don't remember all the young boys. I never met them.

What did he know about the boys? Shush. We don't talk about that. There were many hard things he did each and every day.

Dinner is always very tasty here. I can eat as much as I want. My friends at the table have problems, though. Mary doesn't call me by my right name lots of times. She thinks my name is Julia so I answer to Julia when she calls me Julia. Mary is my good friend even if she doesn't remember to call me by my right name. Mary has been sitting at our table the longest. I don't remember the names of the other two women who sit at our table.

The blonde woman who runs this restaurant is very nice. You can tell she is in charge of the girls who are our waitresses and helpers by the way she talks to them. After dinner most of us go back to the television room and we watch our shows. Sometimes one of the waitresses visits with us and we play word games. I'm very good at word games. Usually we nap for a little while. Sometimes we sing. But that's mostly after lunch. I remember a pretty waitress who used to smile when we sang a song about a beautiful America. Al used to sing in the church choir. He has a deep baritone voice and a wonderful smile. Al hasn't come to visit since I came here.

"How is my favorite patient today, Agnes?"

I don't like some of the priests who come to visit Bishop Jerome. Usually, the Bishop has me sit at his meetings and take shorthand notes. But I'm never allowed in the office when this particular one comes to see my boss. No, he thinks he's so big and important that I can't even be in the same room when he's there. He keeps me out of my Bishop's office. Phooey on him.

"Agnes, do you want a cookie?"

I like this waitress. She always smiles at me. And the cookies are nice and soft. They don't hurt my teeth like the hard, sugary ones. I take my pills with milk. Then she goes and takes orders from other people and I watch our shows.

Al was good with our boy. He played with all the children in the neighborhood. Al is so athletic and good looking. He's going to ask me out on a date one day real soon. I just know it. My father says I should be careful because my boyfriend isn't a Catholic. My mother thinks Al is a very nice young man. I think he's a very nice young man too.

"Bed time, Agnes."

They always come and take me to bed just when I'm getting sleepy.

Every night Al plays with our boy. Our boy. My little beautiful baby.

I miss him so much.

"Brush your teeth, Agnes."

Bishop Jerome has so many things to do. Hospitals and schools to run, speeches to give and buildings to build. During his meetings I sit in a corner of the office and take my notes in my steno book.

"Good morning, Agnes. How are you today?"

Bad man. Bad, bad man. Why do the waitresses let him come

to talk with me? Where are the waitresses?

"You're looking quite well, Agnes, much, much better."

I am supposed to write down everything said during Bishop Jerome's meetings, then type up my shorthand notes. Then I make copies, give one copy to my Bishop, and one copy to Father Mike, Bishop Jerome's Priest secretary. This is what I do. I'm damn good at it. Al and our boy think so too.

"Is everyone treating you well, Agnes? Are the Sisters taking good care of you?"

But not him. When this one came to see my Bishop Jerome, I had to stay at my desk. Father Mike, my Bishop's other secretary, took all the shorthand notes when this bad man came for a meeting with my Bishop.

Bishop Jerome would say, *Sorry, Agnes, clergy business*. My Bishop would say, *How is your boy, Agnes?*

I miss my beautiful boy. He doesn't come to visit. My husband Al is dead.

"Is there anything I can bring you next time I visit?"

You can bring my boy back. That's what you can bring me. No more secrets. I don't want any secrets anymore.

"Would you like more apple juice, Agnes?" I like this one. She has a pretty face and a nice smile. I wish she'd tell me her name.

"Agnes, here, take your pills and drink your juice."

This waitress is a nice one. She has a pretty smile.

Where are the personnel files? Where are the payroll files? Bishop Jerome always asked me when he couldn't find something. Where are the contracts? He has another secretary, Father Mike, besides me, who looks after all of the clerical matters. That is his only job. Father Mike is pretty old. I take care of everything else. All the real diocesan business comes across my desk.

"Come on now, Agnes, take your pills. We'll have cookies in a few minutes, once you've taken your pills."

Inside my Bishop's office was his private filing cabinet.

"Agnes, please, there's nothing for you to get upset about. Take your pills. Be a good girl. We're going to have a sing-along after you take your pills."

This is the nice waitress. She has a lovely singing voice. The apple juice is always cool and the cookies are soft, not the sugary kind which hurt my gums.

Al used to play catch with our boy. They are both such handsome young men. Al's dead. Al plays catch in the backyard with our boy then I call them both in for dinner. When I used to cook. Our house. Al and I had a house. Now I have a room. Al died.

"Time for bed, Agnes. Remember to brush your teeth."

My boy doesn't like priests. *Do I have to go?* I always told him he had to go even when he didn't want to go. Al backs me up on everything when it comes to the Catholic Church.

"How are you today, Agnes?"

Bad man. Bad, bad man.

He came to see my Bishop and I wasn't allowed to be in the room. I'd call Father Mike, the Priest secretary, the old Priest, so he could take notes. There were things my Bishop would only talk about to other priests. Father Mike, borrows steno pads from me but he never returns them.

"Agnes, the Sisters tell me you've been upset lately. Would you like to talk about what's upsetting you?"

Bad man. Bad, bad man. My boy stopped going to church. I'd call him in for dinner but he never came back. Al came in to dinner. Al is a very handsome young man. My mother likes him. My father says Al isn't a Catholic. My father says he doesn't like Al. My father doesn't like my son.

"Good girl, Agnes. Now you can have your cookie."

This one is a happy waitress. I like her. The blonde woman likes her too. They smiled at each other yesterday.

"Time for bed, Agnes. You can watch more shows tomorrow."

Al used to play with our son. Al is dead. Father Mike is dead too. Father Mike and I used to play a game too. We were old then. We could retire soon. We'd make notes in our steno books then we'd trade books and see if we could read what the other had written. This is our secret. I could read his shorthand and Father Mike could read mine. Nobody else in the Bishop's office can read shorthand. And they think they are so smart. They don't know what the funny marks in our steno books mean. They all think computers are clever. Father Mike is a nice old Priest. It's a shame he never had any babies like my son.

"Are you cold, Agnes?"

She's a nice one. She brings the little girl with the tan and white kitty.

"Stay close to me, Agnes. We don't want you to wander away."

It's all very secret.

A few days after we met, Al took me for a walk in the trees. It was summer and we are at young adult camp. Al plays tennis and sings baritone in the camp choir. He is so handsome. He's going to teach me how to play tennis. My mother thinks he's a very nice young man. My father won't let me marry anyone who isn't a Catholic.

Al knows the names of all the trees. He was an Eagle Scout. All the trees have leaves and names when Al is with me. Now they have none.

"Time to go back, Agnes. Don't want you catching cold."

My parents caught colds and died. You'll catch your death. I'm going to marry Al no matter what. Al converted to Catholicism. I am so proud. Shut my father up.

And then my beautiful baby boy. Al is happy. I was happy. Al's dead. Where is our baby?

"Give me your coat, Agnes. Did you have fun outside?"

I like this one. She has a pretty smile.

"Take your pills, Agnes. What a good girl you are."

I am a good girl. That's what my Bishop told me. He is such a brilliant, holy man. Nobody has any idea of all the many problems he solves every day.

"That's my girl, Agnes. Is there anything else you remember?"

Bad man. Bad, bad man. Nothing. Nothing. I'm going to tell you nothing.

"The Sisters say you've been anxious lately, Agnes. What's upsetting you? Please, tell me, Agnes. You'll feel better when you let me know what's bothering you."

A big secret. A big secret between Father Mike and me. And my Bishop. And Al. I had to tell Al. I told Al and now he's dead. And Father Mike is dead too. My Bishop is dead. The Bishop is a handsome man. My mother says Al is a fine young man. Al is taking me to a football game in a few weeks. I have to buy a new hat.

"Where did they play the game, Agnes?"

It's snowing and I'm wearing my new hat. Bad man. Bad, bad man. Nobody ever told me he was a bad priest but I knew. By telling me everything else and the Bishop not telling me about his meetings with this one, I knew. And then Father Mike died. My beautiful baby boy never comes to see me.

"For purple mountain's majesty, above the fruited plane."

I like this one. She has a beautiful voice. Al sings in our church choir. After I told Al the secret, he got sick. Al got sick and died. Al stopped singing.

"Such a darling little kitty, isn't she, Agnes? Yes, you are. Isn't she the most darling little kitty, Agnes?"

Such a pretty little kitty. I like this waitress. She has a happy smile. Not as happy a smile as the little girl's smile but she has a happy smile.

"Theresa couldn't come to visit today but she told me to bring Tabby so Tabby could play her good friend Agnes."

Tabby is tan and white. Patches is black and white. Patches went out one night and never came back. My beautiful baby boy cried. Pretty kitty. You are so warm and cuddly. Yes, you are. You sit on my lap and I'll rub your back. I'll pet you like I pet my baby.

"Take your pills, Agnes. Father says they'll make you feel better. Father wants you to feel better."

I like this waitress. She has a nice smile. Father Mike has a nice smile. Father Mike is old. I'll have to retire soon too. Father Mike and I have secrets. That's why they gave me back all my steno books when Father Mike died. None of them understood what was written in the books. They thought I wrote them. Nobody in the office understands what Father Mike wrote in shorthand except the two of us. My Bishop knew what the books said, I told him.

"Feeling better today, Agnes?"

Father Mike and I are old. My Bishop is a little younger. Not much. All those steno books. Nobody knows how to read shorthand anymore. They think they're so smart. They don't know anything.

A big box. One of the young Priests puts a big box of the steno books Father Mike borrowed from me on my desk.

"What did Father Mike write in all those steno books, Agnes? Was there anything in them the Bishop wanted you to keep secret? You can tell me, Agnes. Bishop Jerome would want you to tell me about everything you read in Father Mike's books. You can trust me, Agnes. Bishop Jerome instructed me to take care of you. Where are Father Mike's steno books, Agnes?"

My boy. My baby. All those names. Father Mike wrote down all the names. All the Priests. All the places. Al never wants to know anything about my job. My Bishop has so many problems to solve each and every day. All the Priests being sent from one parish to another. Some of them go to special houses because they drink too much. All of them drink too much. All the Priests moving here and there because they say they drink too much. Where is my boy? Where is my baby?

"Sister, has Agnes been taking her medication like the good girl she is? You are a good girl, aren't you, Agnes?"

I like this one. She has a pretty smile. Bad, bad man. At Al's funeral, the bad priest took my hand. At Father Mike's funeral the bad priest talked to me. At the Bishop's funeral he wanted me to take a pill. How can a bad priest be a doctor? How can a bad man be a priest? All the priests were transferred to parishes far away then went to solve their drinking problems in places even farther away. All the priests had to go somewhere else. Where is my boy? Where is my baby?

"Take your medicine, Agnes."

Nobody listened to me. Nobody listens to me. So many boys. Father Mike. Father Mike kept all the notes. Father Mike knows it's very, very wrong. Ask Father Mike. My Bishop wants me to keep a secret. He doesn't know about Father Mike's books. I have to tell my Bishop about Father Mike's steno books.

My boy. He comes to visit me at work on Wednesdays. He has only half a day of school on Wednesdays. He is so young and handsome. He shakes hands with my Bishop Jerome and the other priests. Eleven years old and he already knows enough to assist at the Mass. One of the Fathers helps him with his studies during the afternoons when I have to be at my desk. I am so happy my baby can come here and have a Father look after him.

"Has she been in this state for long, Sister?"

I knew it. I knew it. I knew it. I knew it.

"Father, Agnes is entering stage three. She's not responding to her current dosage."

"Well, we'll have to give our dear Agnes a little more. We don't want her to feel any discomfort at all. Now do we, Agnes?"

I saw it all in my boy's eyes. I knew it. And I kept sending him back. He'd never say anything. My baby. All the priests on Father Mike's list. They were the ones who were so nice and wanting to spend time with my baby. I knew it. I knew it. I didn't stop it. I didn't know. I knew it.

"Will this prescription help, Father?"

He hates me. My beautiful little baby hates me. I sat there all day surrounded by those priests. I sent my son to them. Forgive me.

"Sister, dementia in this form doesn't respond to any of our known treatments. All we can do is continue with our current medications and make sure Agnes remains as comfortable as possible."

Father Mike's books. Why did I tell my Bishop and not the police? Why did I bring my only son? Why did I work for them for my entire life? Oh, God, no.

"Here you go, Agnes. Father says this will help you feel better."

Help me. Please. Somebody help me. Where is my baby? Al, please help me. Please somebody please help me. My son. They let me sacrifice my only son.

"Good girl, Agnes. Would you like a cookie? It's the soft kind. The kind you like."

I like this waitress. She has a pretty smile. I like it here. I can eat as much as I want. Al is a handsome young man. He's going to bring me to a football game soon. We have a young baby. He is very smart. Our baby serves at daily Mass. So many of the priests say he's such a beautiful little boy.

God help me.

SOLITAIRE QUARTET

LADIES AND GENTLEMEN! I want to thank all of you for coming here this evening! And the management of the Club Zichawawa wants you to know that they hope YOUR three glamorous days and exciting nights will be the most fabulous of YOUR life! Thank-you.   TONIGHT! Oh, tonight, and for that matter, ALL WEEKEND!, we have something very special for all of you card fanciers out there. We have been BLESSED! And I do mean BLESSED! by the International Gaming Commission with the opportunity to be this year's host for the fourth annual, INTERNATIONAL SOLITAIRE FINALS!!! Yeah! You know it! Thank-you. Thank-you so very, very much.

So without further ado, I would like to introduce you to the finalists, who have come here, to ATLANTIC CITY!!, from virtually the four corners of the WORLD!! Thank-you. From Great Britain, we have the greater pleasure of introducing, MR. IAN HOLLISTER!! Mr. Hollister.

Thank-you. It is a great pleasure to be representing all of my solitaire playing countrymen at this tournament this evening.

Thank-you. And now, from the People's Republic of CHINA!!, we are happy to introduce to you, MR. LAO TZE GHUNG!!! Who although used to playing a somewhat modified version of the game we're playing in this tournament, - We won't say who's right this evening. Thank-you. - has told us privately - As much of a secret as we can keep, eh, Mr. Ghung! Thank-you. - that he has been preparing for this match with an even greater fervor than that which he brought to the championship representing over one quarter of the population of THIS PLANET!! And that's some sort of fervor! Thank-you. And now, MR. GHUNG!

Thank-you. Hello. I am honored to be here.

Thank-you, Mr. Ghung. Pleasure to have you with us this evening. Our third finalist is MRS.....

Let's see now. This one goes there and over here to there. Flip. Good. O.K., what's going on down there? Shit. That's not going to be doing anybody too much good even if I can dig it out later. Not bad. Looks like this might be going somewhere for a change. What's the score? Where can those damn twos be? There's nothing worse than having all of those damn aces up there sitting around doing nothing and those damn twos lost somewhere in the ozone. Here, twos! Gotcha! You little spade bum. No offense meant. I've gotta be out of my mind talking to a card like that. Nothing but a card. Aha! Showing you that I'm a liberal here's that little bastard of a diamond. Good. Three. Four. What's the count? Nine. With three more under and an open ace. Good. Keep it open and you can start rebuilding the bank. Damn! Well, alright. Eleven. Give me that last ace and we'll walk out of here in roses. Hot damn. It's still a winner but... Good. Nobody else hit for the big one. Well, ALRIGHT!

There was always basketball. Rules changed over the last forty years, but the game is still the same. Back then the emphasis of the game was different. Everybody was around the same size. What the hell. All that really matters is how fast you are. You have to be faster then some turkey who happens to be 7'2". And you're only 5'8". A lot faster. Sure. Back then Digger played for any team that would have him. He'd remember how they used to come out on those Saturday afternoons to watch the way all the young men could run around for hours and still have a good time. And when it clicked. What else could there be? During the week when they didn't get as many spectators it was sometimes even better. Get up in the morning around six or seven. Put in your ten hours running paperwork around the office. Play a couple of hours of b-ball. Go out for a couple of beers. Good night's sleep and then work again in the morning. You felt fine and life was worth living. Not too many people take sports that way anymore. Too busy watching some overpaid jerk on the TV. Too much pressure for success.

When Digger played the game if some fool was all over your back, you went outside for a couple of minutes and worked things out. Then you went back in and got back to the game. No hard feelings. Just working off a little extra energy. Wherever he'd gotten the extra energy.

You got the same ten dollars whether you won or lost. There was no reason to go around busting heads. Well, maybe now and then, but the teams stuck together even if they hardly knew each other off the court. It was the game and a good way to get some exercise while you waited for the baseball season to start. But all of that had been a long time ago. Now it's the International Solitaire Championship taking up all his time. Digger is ready to expend the supreme effort. That feeling within when all his being is working toward that one supreme goal which he understands completely. Where he knows all of the rules. And all the moves.

Trees uprooted the sidewalks years ago. Brownstone homes on a street which gave all its life to a war. There were jobs and good times but now was the time to move on. The buildings were falling apart and he was priced out of the city. They sold houses cheap in the country. The kids should grow up breathing clean country air. He'd been born and raised three blocks away. All his life was here. He had to go. There really was no choice.

Saturday afternoon is the time for a last trip back. Pack what you can into the car and kiss the rest goodbye. There isn't much going on where he's going but this time the moves aren't there. He could go anywhere from this point and it would be the same. Cities were fun while he was growing up but why should his kids have to put up with the aggravation? Kids can have fun no mater where they are. It's part of their metabolism.

LADIES AND GENTLEMEN!! The results from the first round of play are now in. We find the leader at this point in the competition to be, the distinguished representative from the Republic of Tibet, MR. VAUGHN VINH, with the amazing winnings of OVER ONE HUNDRED AND THREE THOUSAND DOLLARS!!!. Thank-you.

Deal them cards. Now that's an occupation to be desired,

especially when you don't have any other occupation handy. It's a bear trying to make any money at all playing solitaire. Just once to sit at a blackjack table and put all the money on one small hand of cards. And to take this damn casino to the laundry. Put 'em in your back pocket. Put 'em to the wall. The odds are a hell of a lot better than the game he's playing now. Had to be.

Digger'd even heard of people actually winning at blackjack. Nobody ever won at solitaire. Patience. The game sounds great to him. Sitting at the main table in one of those ornate casinos, throwing money around like Donald Trump. What the hell. It's only money. Besides, we're winning. Brand new suit. Buy a really expensive car. House up in the mountains and an apartment in the city. Can't miss.

Never could happen. But if it did it couldn't miss. Sitting there having all of those people gawk at you while you toss thousands of dollars on the table. Money they can only imagine ever having for themselves. What else can you expect from the fantasies of a solitaire player?

But this is a complicated game. The only one where you not only knew you eventually were going to lose; you knew you were going to lose virtually ever hand dealt to you. Nothing's better than when you win.

Cards come to you as if they're following the pattern of your dreams. You make the wish for one card and it leads to three you desired even more. Those three fall into place, and as you reach for another, you know it will make the hand even more beautiful.

And then they will all line up. Every card in its assigned place. Like troops to be reviewed, as you stand on the balcony waving to them in your uniform with the braid running down its side, telling them the new day is at hand.

For all of us it will be a time of hard work and tears, but soon, so very soon, we will have only memories of this rubble all around us. Here we shall rebuild this war ravaged city. And the people cheer and call up to you on your balcony.

It is good to see all of them like this. Happy and content. But there is work left to be done and you retire to your office to draw the plans for the new age. With a sweep of your hand creating a new dam to irrigate the northern valley. With a word setting in motion the research that will eventually improve the health and quality of life for all your people. It will be good.

In the evening you see an opera, at least part of the first act, as you become drowsy during the climactic scenes. You will rule and all of the cards will be shuffled.

Coffee has to be made. Digger looks around the kitchen. It isn't clean but it isn't all that dirty. It's time for a break. There are lots of perfect games but he didn't come across one every day. Why not celebrate? Digger finds himself staring out the window. The front yard is covered with a thin layer of melting snow. There isn't a damn thing going on in the street. Two o'clock in the afternoon. All the kids are still in the split level school. What can he do? He remembers a few moves to the hoop and goes through the ritual pantomime. A quick jump. The ball bounces off the backboard and begins circling the rim. The ball spins on the rim for a few moments before dropping through the hoop. A perfect solitaire.

But what's the use? Digger pours himself a cup of coffee. His wife will be home soon. He thinks about making dinner.

Thank-you. Thank-you, very much. The results from the final round are now coming in from the main room. Yes. And here they are. In third place, we have the outstanding player from that little island in the Pacific we all know and love, the multi-talented representative from Guam, MR. ACHED WILIDONKA!! Mr. Wilidonka.

I am very pleased to have done so well in such talented company.

Thank you, Mr. Wilidonka. Mr. Ached Wilidonka, ladies and gentlemen. And now from that land of canals and chocolate, in second place, Mr....

Digger boils some water. The game will continue tomorrow.

MR. PERSONALITY

"That's MISTER Personality to you, pal. Any other questions?"

"Mr. Personality! Mr. Personality!"

"Yeah, young lady in third row." Standing at the podium, the Big Man points to one of the gathered news crews.

"Mr. Personality, now that you're no longer hosting the radio show, how are you going to fill your spare time?"

"Glad you asked that question. Paula, it is Paula, isn't it?"

"Yes, Mr. Personality."

"Well, Paula, as you well know, as all of you know I'm sure, I've been broadcasting to the American people for over twenty years. Saying goodbye to my audience is one of the hardest things I'll ever have to do in my life.

"Now, the good folks out there in what I fondly refer to as "America's Radioland" have been listening to what I've had to say; what I consider honest, middle American, rock solid, straight down the middle, and as Patriotic as I can make it; my opinions, for over twenty years, and I think it's time for me to move to something else. Something where my vast radio experience and solid American values will be appreciated by a wider, ever increasing, audience."

"Mr. Personality, does this mean you'll be running for future political office? Or will we be seeing you somewhere else in show business?"

"Well, Paula, the great one, the Gipper, himself, once said. I'm pretty sure he said it. You guys know how accurate I can be with quotes. Well, the big fella was at dinner one night with some of the most powerful, most influential folks in government and business, and some pipsqueak reporter came up to him in the middle of dessert and asked the big man, Ronnie Reagan himself, if he had to choose one career for his entire life, one or the other, exclusive, which career would he have stayed with, acting or politics?

"Well, ole Ronnie looks the kid reporter straight in the eye, takes a three count for dramatic effect, and, summoning up all the gravity he could with both his legendary voice and his classic stern expression, leans in to the kid and Reagan deadpans, 'You mean there's a difference?'

"Got to love it. Don't you?"

"Mr. Personality! Mr. Personality! Another question, please, Mr. Personality!"

"Sorry, guys. It's been a long day and, with any luck, we've all got another long one coming up tomorrow. Goodnight!"

And that was that. Mr. Personality made his way off stage after announcing his retirement from twenty years of radio broadcasting over the nation's airwaves. In those two decades he'd made and broken politicians of all stripes, launched careers of mediocrities simply because they performed as exceptional radio guests, and harassed and hounded hundreds of liberal lefties from academia to the Pentagon. Close to thirty million people hung on his golden words each and every day. And now he was calling it a career, moving on to greener pastures, wherever they turned out to be.

Pulling up to the gate, Mr. Personality punches numbers into the touchpad. Security specialists insisted he put a wall around his estate when a couple of years back, Mr. Personality came home one evening to find three underage girls in various states of undress, lounging about his kitchen. Fortunately for the conservative voice of America, Linda Lewis was firmly attached to Mr. Personality's arm that evening and as they both whipped out their cell phones, help from Mr. Personality's security firm and the local gendarmes was on its way before the three nymphets were able to compromise Mr. Personality's public persona any more than twenty years on top of the ratings had already done.

So that's why the gate, which Mr. Personality, with a click of his remote control, closes behind him as he continues up the half mile driveway leading to the manor house. Manor house was the way he referred to his home on the radio whenever the subject arose. Owning a manor house became part and parcel of Mr. Personality's radio persona He could talk about lazy, shiftless welfare mothers and the men who mooched necessities from them, partially because he lived in a manor house. He'd started from nowhere and now lived like a king. To his listeners who identified with him in toto, who dreamt of being like him, of being able to speak for hours on any subject, of being prosperous enough to live in a manor house, to know enough to cure the aggravations of everyday life if only those in power would remove their boot from the neck of everyday Joe's like them, Mr. Personality was the fulfillment of the American dream. And Mr. Personality lived in a grand gated estate to prove it.

"More, Mr. P?" Lilliana Lopes held the pitcher of protein fortified smoothies inches from her boss's goblet.

Shaking his head, Mr. Personality used the hand not holding the phone to shoo his housekeeper away. His doctor told him to knock off phone calls while he ate dinner but business remained business and being a radio talk show host, much like being a telephone solicitor, meant you spend time on the phone while most people are enjoying a quiet dinner. Mr. P knew to catch his sources during one of the most vulnerable parts of their day.

"Glad to be of what help I can be, Senator."

Instead of moving away, Lilliana held her ground, scowling at her employer.

"Television is a new medium for me, Senator. You give me a couple of weeks to get my sea legs and once that happens, I can assure you, the Mr. Personality machine will once again be firing on all cylinders." Hearing something out of the ordinary, Mr. P stops staring at his own cuticles and glances up to his employee.

With a heavy hand Lilliana parked the pitcher on the elongated dining room table. She folds her arms and even with his good ear plugged into his cell phone, Mr. P heard the tapping of Lilliana's shoe against the perfectly buffed teak floor boards.

"Right. Then Monday night it is. We're going to give them hell, that's for sure, Senator. Goodnight now."

"Take your pills, Mr. P, you know how you get when you wait to take them too long."

This was their evening routine. Ever since Mr. Personality sponsored Lilliana and her daughter's visa applications, and the two took up permanent residence in the mansion, more and more his life had fallen under his housekeeper's influence. In a way they controlled him as much as he controlled them. With contacts achieved over twenty years of broadcasting, both Lilliana and her child could be back on a plane to Asia with one phone call, should their boss ever fall into such a black mood as to order it done. But he would never do such a thing. Mother and daughter, even as a young man he'd dared not imagine.

But Lilliana maintained her weapons of mutual destruction as well.

When Lilliana and her daughter were delivered to the doorstep of the nation's radio host, Linda Lewis was still firmly attached to Mr. Personality's arm. As consort-in-chief to the Conservative spokesperson for moral values within the United States of America, not only did Linda Lewis maintain a low profile, she needed to assure that all those coming into contact with the Man were of impeccable character and willing to sacrifice themselves for the sake of Mr. Personality, should need arrive.

And Linda Lewis oversaw the vetting of her Star's inner circle. Over the course of six years, Linda Lewis managed to fire Mr. Personality's personal manager, change the law office which handled the many frivolous business lawsuits any public person was subjected to without real cause year in and year out, drop his accountants, and strongly suggest that a number of Mr. P's relatives go out and get real work since the gravy train would no longer make station stops in their neighborhood.

And Linda Lewis was just the person to take on such daunting tasks. She'd first met Mr. Personality when he was a mere regional radio hit. Back then his show consisted of pure vitriol aimed at an audience whose functional literacy level would have been the lowest tested across the radio dial, if anyone bothered to make such a survey. He talked hate to those left behind in life, to those who thought they'd been left behind for no good reason other than blacks, hispanics, immigrants, or whoever else was the target of the week, taking away their birthright.

Linda Lewis imagined Mr. Personality's typical audience member to be a lower middle class, White male stiff, stuck in traffic on his way to another meaningless day on the job where pressures on him were immeasurable. Alone in his automobile, frustrated, literally at every turn, ideal radio listener is tuned into Mr. Personality's radio show where Mr. Personality directs the rage of his audience. Where else can both suburban commuters and urban factory workers vent their frustrations? Certainly not on the job. Their work places are more tightly regulated than any despot's wet dream. Joe Radiolistener's phone conversations are intermittently monitored at work. His e-mails considered company property and perused by higher ups at will. Ditto for snail mail. Idle conversations in break rooms can be reported by company spies and charges brought against him for even the most innocuous conversations. And that's just on the job.

Home life isn't any improvement. Aside from being second mortgaged up to his ears, Joe Radiolistener has to keep up with classic domestic dilemmas. He lives in a historic fantasy world where white men ruled supreme, sometime way back when. When a white man spoke, the wife would keep quiet and obey, the kids would go to their rooms and do their homework and not give him any lip, and his neighbors had the same coloration and held the same opinions. Fantasyland. That's the land where Linda Lewis made sure Mr. Personality sold acreage to his listeners. Prime lots in Fantasyland.

What Linda Lewis understood, and she was never quite sure Mr. Personality grasped the concept himself, what Linda Lewis understood was that this white male, lower middle class fantasy only existed in the cars Joe Radiolistener drove to work every day, five days a week, fifty weeks a year.

Bread and circuses. Old as the hills but the formula works. Corporations now made sure workers received enough to keep them from understanding how little they were getting, while simultaneously underwriting entertainers like Mr. Personality to deflect the rage and turmoil Joeradiolistener experiences but can't coherently express.

Christians to the lions. That's the way. Mr. Personality decided who would be the sacrificial Christians each week, maintaining a reliable entertainment flow to his Coliseum of the airwaves.

"Don't you just love it the way these mealy mouth intellectuals think nobody should have to work for anything and the government is simply going to tell you, you the working man of America, how much of your hard earned money, your blood, sweat and tears, your paycheck, you get to keep each week? I mean really, do they think we're such a fools as not to notice we're working five months out of each and every year so some limp wristed, Washington bureaucrat, can crawl back to his masters and report exactly how much he's screwing you and every working man and woman in America? Get with it, my friend. Do you think for one single moment, for the tiniest sliver of time, man, and modern day science, has ever measured, a micro-second, a mini-mini-micro-second, do you think that for this infinitely tiny bit of time, do you think that those limp-wristed, skinny necked, pencil pushing bureaucrats sitting back there in Washington, care, for the tiniest sliver of time, about the needs and wants of your average working man in America? Do they care about your mortgage, the money you pay for little Johnny's orthodontist? Do you think they care about all the hard earned cash you have to pay for little Sally, so she and your other kids can attend a good school, because the public schools have gotten so far out of hand in denying the existence of an Almighty God, and insisting homosexuals be hired as teachers in the classroom to indoctrinate children into perversities too unimaginable for me even to speak about over these, our public airwaves?

"Let me tell you, right now. Are you listening to me out there? Well, sit up straight and pay attention. Let me tell you, right now, how much those limp-wristed, skinny necked bureaucrats back there in those plush, high rise, office buildings in Washington care about the needs and aspirations of the common working man today in this great United States of America. They don't care at all. How each working day they try to figure out how much pain they can inflict on you and me each time they force another one of those unnecessary regulations and laws down our throats. You want to know how much time they think about working stiffs like you and me? I'll tell you how much time they spend thinking about the common folk. Zero. Nil. Zip. Nada. Squat. Goose egg. The big slide. Nothing. Not a second of the government's time is spent caring about how what they do, the regulations they write, the laws they pass, will effect you and me, our families and our children. They could care less about how what they do effects the common man as long as they can increase, their power, within their own sycophantic departments. How they can improve their own positions inside the government. That's all they ever think about. Twenty-four hours a day. Seven days a week. Fifty-two weeks out of the year. They don't even take time off for vacations, when it comes to getting ahead and improving their positions, their select sinecures, in government. That's what we're all up against, folks. It's a hard row we've got to hoe. Don't think for a second the government is going to lend a hand to help you out. No help for any of us wage slaves. Thousands of bureaucrats lining their own pockets at your expense. Think about it. Think about it every time you look at your pay stub and see how much of your money, your money, ladies and gentlemen, is going to the thin neck pencil pushers in Washington D. C.. Think about this the next time you're buying groceries at the supermarket, you just count up how much extra you have to pay in sales tax after they've already over taxed you on your paycheck. Think about it, my fellow Americans. Double, triple taxation. We've all got a lot of work to do if we're ever going to dig ourselves out of the deep, deep hole our government has dug for all of us. Think about it."

This was one of Mr. Personality's patented rants. Linda Lewis, in her position as Executive Producer of the Mr. Personality radio talkshow, tried to keep his rants in a logical rotation.

Quitting booze hadn't been as hard as Mr. Personality thought it would be. Pills certainly helped and helped keep the weight off as well. Sitting under the heat lamps set up alongside his indoor pool, he enjoys a short respite between shutting down his radio show and starting a new career as the conservative conscience of American cable television.

"Lilliana, where's my medication?"

Damn. Never around when you want her to be and when she is around, never leaves until you tell her fifteen times to get out.

"Lilliana, medication, chop, chop."

Put her back on a plane to Manila, or wherever she came from.

"Mr. P, you want me? Right now?"

Oh, crap, here it comes again. Try to get a little service around here and all I get is the pitiful sex toy routine.

"Prescription, Lilliana, get me more of my prescription, now."

Mr. Personality's housekeeper turns her back on her boss and goes back into the great room. She grabs her jacket off the hook and heads into the garage. Mr. Personality listens as she starts the car and pulls out into the drive.

"And get back soon. I don't have all day to waste." Not that she possibly could hear.

She hasn't been the same since her daughter took off. You'd think she'd have more respect. After all, if Mr. Personality hadn't sponsored her visa application, she'd be hanging around some dive in the middle of the jungle pushing herself or her daughter on whoever coughed up the price of a couple of handfuls of rice, or whatever they eat around there. Nerve of some people, once they set foot in America, they forget planes fly in both directions.

Mr. Personality's phone rang again.

How did they get the new number so fast? Another topic to discuss with Lilliana. Probably worth a couple of grand for her to hand over his home phone number to one of the tabloid reporters who'd pay anything to uncover real dirt on Mr. Personality.

"Who the hell is this?"

"Simmer down, big guy, checking in to see how retirement's treating you."

Linda Lewis, agent, manager, confidant, Mr. P knows she has enough on him to sink him. Same as he could she. "What's up, sweets?"

"Wanted to let you know, you might not want to send your housekeeper out for any more goodies from the quicki-mart."

"Come again."

"Well, how should I put this over a cell phone, well, the manager of the quicki-mart went on a sabbatical upstate. For a couple of years."

"And his store's been shut down?"

"Well, big guy, not exactly. I'm told the competition took over the location and is not being nice to his old customers. If you know what I mean."

Click. Or whatever sound a cell phone makes when you hang up.

Nothing. Out of range or not in service. Mr. P tries again to connect with his housekeeper. If Mr. Personality got out of his chair and went to the kitchen he'd probably find Lilliana's cell phone, battery dead, on the counter, where she usually left it. "But if I take it with me I might lose it." Her logic was flawless if not completely inane. He tries the number again. Same result. Time to cover all the bases.

"Bill, if you could find some time in the next hour or two, I'd like you to come by the house so we can have a little chat."

Lawyers, guns and money. Bill the Lawyer takes care of the first part. Same way he'd been taking care of Mr. P for the past six years, ever since syndication started paying the star bucks and demanding a lawyer who knew how to negotiate a star's contracts.

Lawyers.

Guns.

"Howard, how are you this evening?" Security became necessary along with the nationwide audience. His estate's grounds were under constant electronic surveillance, interior security can be activated by the flick of a switch, and armed patrols cruised the surrounding area at staggered intervals. "Howard, tomorrow or the next day, I'm moving to my country place for an extended stay. I'd like to maintain my privacy while I'm down there. How about sending a few of your people over to make sure everything stays civilized."

Money.

Money's the easy part. Krugerrands at every residence. Diamonds in the safe. Internet connections to offshore banks. Mr. Personality makes his way into the den and types commands into the computer. Clear out as much as possible and transfer the majority of his holdings to off-shore accounts. He'd been assured it would take years for any government agency to trace where the money went from there. Sometimes it's a good thing listening to paranoid right wing conspiracy theorists day-in and day-out.

What happened in the next few hours would be crucial.

Scenario Number One: Lilliana calls her boss from a pay phone and tells him his connection has changed locations and asks what to do next. No harm, no foul.

Scenario Number Two: Lilliana calls her boss from the local police station house wanting to be bailed out. Send Bill the Lawyer and have them both try very hard to keep Mr. P's name out of everything. Try very, very hard to keep Mr. P's name out of it.

Scenario Number Three: Lilliana returns to the manor house with the usual bag of pills and hands them over to Mr. Personality. Everything Mr. Personality says and does will then be taped and filmed by Federal narcotics officers and after a few weeks of this, the Feds raid the manor house, arrest Mr. Personality and use Lilliana as their primary witness against her boss. Mr. P ends up doing three years mandatory hard time.

Wait and see. Wait and see. Lilliana's been gone over half an hour. What's her usual time for one of these runs? Hour? Hour-and-a-half? Better get packing.

Doorbell. Bill the Lawyer? Security people? Lilliana would let herself in, that's for sure. Narcs? Would they ring the bell? Mr. Personality's stomach does a 360. Nothing he can do about this. Everything's already in motion.

"Mr. Personality, do you have anything to say regarding an indictment drawn up against you by Federal prosecutors, concerning possession and distribution of illegal narcotics? Will you be hiring lawyers to quash any subpoenas the Drug Enforcement Administration may issue?"

Mr. P should pay more attention to incoming phone calls. Having a face-to-face with the fourth estate is not the best way to budget time. There's no good way to answer these questions. Where the hell is Lilliana with my prescription?

"Do you have a cigarette?"

A long time ago Mr. P learned how to work the press. Give them a little something, "Mr. P smokes cigs on the sly." Promise them future access. Make them think they're entering the inner circle when you invite them for a scotch and a nosh.

"Your housekeeper claims you sent her out to buy black market opiates from neighborhood drug dealers. Is there any truth to claims you are addicted to the drug oxycodin and you use your household employees as mules to purchase them illegally?"

Yada, yada, yada, yada. Where the hell is Lilliana with his prescription. It's my back, if I don't have my prescription, my back will start to hurt.

"Mr. Personality, do you have a response to your housekeeper's claims, Lilliana Lopes? Does Lilliana Lopes work for you?"

One of these days, you're going to miss me. One of these days. "Yes, Lilliana works for me. Is there some kind of a problem?" Do I know this guy? "Are you going to be photographing me? If you are, I should freshen up a bit."

Mr. Personality feels an adrenaline surge crash through his body. Like a wave cascading though his stomach, shaking his chest, pulsing past his neck. "I have to sit down."

Reaching for the door frame, Mr. Personality slowly lowers his body to the floor.

"You alright?"

"I have to lie down for a little bit. Don't worry about me. I'll be fine in a second." Sitting on the floor, Mr. P waves away the reporter as he bends over and offers a hand. "Just give me a couple of seconds here and I'll be fine. Let's keep this between the two of us and I'll treat you right."

Where the hell is Lilliana and my pills?

Sure is comfortable down here. No reason to get up. Lie down. Have a good rest.

"You doing OK down there, Mr. Personality?"

Damn. This is embarrassing. "Do you have a camera?" Why bother? I'm going to lie down here a little bit longer.

"Should I call 9-1-1?"

Now hold on there a second, fella.

Mr. Personality now knew he had to stand up. Didn't matter that he felt more comfortable sitting on the floor. Can't have some liberal do-gooder calling in an ambulance or the police and having everybody taking pictures of Mr. Personality when they wheel him into the ambulance.

"Can I help you up?"

Get it together. Get it together. Show time. Suck it up. It's all part of being an adult. When you feel like lying down, you have to stand up straight, suck in your stomach, push out your chest and face life like a man. Time to get up. Get up, Mr. Personality, rise and shine. Work to be done, day's challenges to meet.

There you go. Only a little lightheadedness.

"Come in. Come in. Only give me a minute if you will. Low blood sugar. Come in. I'll be with you in a minute."

Rising to his full height, the big man felt good enough to release his grip from the doorframe and lead his guest across the great room and into the kitchen. "Give me a second here. Some orange juice should help." As Mr. Personality heads to the refrigerator, the reporter takes his notebook out of his pocket and seats himself at the counter to begin an interview.

"Mr. Personality, how long have you been addicted to opiate drugs? And when do you intend to commit yourself to a treatment center?"

Orange juice, top shelf. Glass. Grab a glass. Open half-gallon carton of juice. Steady. Pour the juice.

I'm going down.

This time when Mr. Personality hit the floor, two quarts of orange juice hit the floor with him.

HEAL THYSELF

"Early reports estimate those in attendance to be anywhere from eight to ten thousand." With tape recorder rolling and camera clicking off frames, the Reporter makes notes for tomorrow's story.

From his position in the stands, the Reporter opens his lens for wide shots of the end zone where electricians still work on last minute adjustments to the stage's sound system. Where a community college seven weekends a year plays football, now thousands gather to hear voices of governmental opposition.

"Tonight's rally came close to being canceled owing to a restraining order issued late last night. Citing threats of violence to some of the speakers and questions regarding the rally's permits, a circuit court Judge issued the restraining order.

"Late this afternoon yesterday's restraining order was overturned by the Superior Court citing freedom of speech and assembly. Security remains tight as those attending tonight's rally continue to stream into the stands and onto the field."

Moving down from his position in the bleachers, the Reporter enters the field house behind the stage.

"Time, Doctor, it's time."

They begin to walk. A few paces ahead, Security elbows their way through the crowded hallway, clearing a path for the evening's featured speaker. All eyes focus on the Doctor, but his face reveals nothing.

Sliding in behind the security cordon, the Reporter manages to ask a quick question. "What extra precautions are you taking in response to today's events?"

The Doctor nods to the Reporter and continues on his way.

Taking a sharp right on to a suburban tree lined street, the Driver slows the station wagon as he reads mailbox numbers. His Passenger holds a small package wrapped in brown paper "Keep going. I'll tell you when to stop."

From the opposite direction a slow moving newspaper delivery truck passes the two men by. A young boy stands in the bed of the pickup tossing the morning paper at front doors. Opening his window, the Passenger motions the Driver to roll his down as well. "We need some fresh air. Pure fresh air."

The Passenger taps his fingers on the package in his lap. "Praise be."

Stationed on rooftops surrounding the athletic field, police snipers and their spotters monitor the crowd as it assembles. As he approaches the stage, the Inspector scans the eyes and hands of those closest to him. Uniformed officers stand positioned, surrounding the stage and scattered every thirty yards or so throughout the crowd. Tonight's audience has already filled a dozen rows of bleacher seats and begins streaming on to the grass immediately in front of the stage.

Outside this small stadium, the parking lot has few spots remaining and the attendants begin turning away cars.

Reaching the stage, the Inspector turns and counts those officers stationed on rooftops. He smiles toward their binoculars, knowing full well the destructive tools these men carry.

"And you're here for the Doctor's speech?" With three cameras strapped to his body, the Reporter wields a fourth as he snaps person-in-the-street head shots.

"My wife and family came tonight to make sure everyone

knows this Doctor for the murderer he is. He's guilty of genocide. He deserves the death penalty for those innocent lives he's taken. Make sure you put in your paper that honest, good people came here tonight to bear witness against this criminal."

Backing away, the Reporter goes for a wide shot to include the dozen or so demonstrators carrying similar signs. They all demand the Doctor at best be imprisoned, at worst, shot on sight. The Reporter raises his voice to be heard from his new distance, "Deserves to be executed? Is your organization going to carry out the Doctor's execution?"

"That's not for us here to do. The Lord will see all killers of innocents punished. We're here taking advantage of our Constitutional freedoms of speech and assembly. We've elected true Christians to run this country. They'll take care of the Doctor and his colleagues soon enough. We came here in peace to bear witness. We are completely non-violent."

On the sidewalk, brushing creases from his stolen uniform, the Passenger reads from a clipboard in his left hand. He approaches the split-level ranch home looking, if anyone interested, like just another deliveryman.

As he reaches the front door, he feigns ringing its bell, waits a few seconds, then repeats his charade. He checks his watch and taps his foot. Finally, he places the brown paper package on a mat next to the door. The Passenger scribbles a few words on his clipboard, turns, and heads back to the station wagon.

"Everything okay?" Shifting gears, the Driver pulls away from the curb.

"Package delivered." All buckled up, the Passenger makes a sign of the cross.

"Praise the Lord." After five minutes of cruising through suburban neighborhoods, the station wagon finds a highway's on ramp and is soon far away.

From her desk, the Commissioner's secretary waves the Inspector into the inner office.

Seated behind her desk, the Commissioner raises her head to the Inspector. "You'll be running tonight's security detail." As the Commissioner looks directly into her underling's eyes, she licks an envelope flap, seals it, then flips it into the out-tray.

"We're proceeding on schedule. This morning's incident increased anxiety all around. But we are ready." The Inspector lifts his chin and looks down toward his boss.

"Do you have the operatives you'll need?" Leaning back in her chair, the Commissioner motions the Inspector to take a seat.

"Breakfast. Get a move on. Your father's already left." An egg salad sandwich is entombed within a baggie as the Wife slips it into one of two thermal lunch sacks.

"I'm here. Let's eat." The Boy takes a seat at the breakfast table, and pours a glass of orange juice.

"I'll be right down. I'm cleaning Budgie's cage." Soon footsteps clatter down stairs and after a few moments the Daughter enters the breakfast area carrying a brown paper sack. She puts it into the garbage receptacle under the sink. She squirts some hand soap into her palm.

Without looking up from her lunch work the Wife instructs the Daughter. "Wash your hands."

Shrugging her shoulders the Daughter looks to her brother. As she turns on the tap, both twins recite in unison, "Yes, Mother."

"Another route this morning?" From the back seat, the Doctor engages in ritual daily small talk with the Bodyguard. For the Doctor, such niceties are a struggle.

"Well, Doc, after I saw you carrying out that stinky old garbage, I didn't think you'd want me to drive you through any neighborhood where they'd be able to put your face to the scent. Right?" As the Bodyguard talks, he waves his right hand in the air and steers the car with his left.

"A doctor's work in never done." And that ends the morning small talk. Opening his briefcase, the Doctor skims medical journals as the Bodyguard turns on a national news program. Both men settle in for the now routine forty-five minute commute to the clinic.

"One day we will all be called to answer for our time here on earth, and how we use our time, from this moment on, is how we'll be judged." Ordinarily, during this part of his sermon the Preacher's voice would be roaring full blast, but considering the hour, location, and paucity of his congregation, as he turns his body around in the driver's seat, his voice barely rises above a whisper.

Inside the panel van, Driver, Passenger and the Third Person stretch out quietly as the Preacher speaks. Semi-tractor trailers surround them and the sounds of vehicles merging onto the interstate along with slamming car doors find there way into the cargo compartment. The three hadn't met before this evening. The Preacher knows them all. Only he knows their names and how they can be reached.

"This morning's action could well be the last engagement of our long campaign,"

"I've heard that before." Shifting his legs, the Third Person crosses one over the other. "Accomplishing goals isn't comforting for folks in my line of work."

"Your career choice is not our subject of discussion at the moment." The Preacher now looks through the van's windshield.

"What instructions I've received indicate our operation will be mothballed following today's delivery. We've accomplished many of our goals and now our political arm wishes that we retire for the foreseeable future."

"They've sold out. 100% sold out. We weren't supposed to stop until we'd shut them all down. Sold out for political office. It's crap." The Passenger motions the Third Person to hand him the package. "We saw this coming."

The Preacher gazes through the windshield.

"Do you have to speak tonight, honey?" Pulling her skirt into position, the Wife finishes dressing.

After lacing his running shoes, the Doctor follows the Wife downstairs to the kitchen. "It's not a big thing. No need to worry. I'm only one of a dozen or so people on the bill."

"You really don't have to do it." They bring bowls, silverware, milk and juice to the table. The Doctor makes coffee. The Wife fries eggs.

"I'm not trying to be a hero. It's part of the job. You know it and I know it. I'll have protection."

"Don't count on them for anything. Stay with our people."

They eat in silence.

They hear a car horn.

"I've got to go." The Doctor kisses the Wife and heads to the front door.

"Wait." The Wife wipes eggs from her mouth. "Did you take out the cans last night?"

Shrugging his shoulders, the Doctor reverses course and goes to the interior garage door. "A doctor's work is never done."

"Well it would be if he'd done it last night."

"Later." Stepping into the attached garage, the Doctor wheels a trash container to the curb as the Bodyguard advances the car twenty yards from end of the walkway to the end of the driveway where the Doctor parks the garbage bin.

"Morning, Doc, you study a lot of years for that job?"

The Inspector recognizes fifteen to twenty men as they approach the stage. For a crowd this size, the Inspector would have booked a larger venue, but you never know how many people will show for any particular events like this.

Numbers are always a question. This field can easily hold ten thousand but tonight it looks like more than that. There's a list of speakers as long as the Inspector's arm. He doesn't know exactly who the target will be, but he has a good idea.

Make sure operatives are in place. Check for anything appearing out of the ordinary. Leave before the program begins and be at the precinct, sitting at a desk, when the phones start ringing.

Dozens of costumed demonstrators make their way to a position directly below the stage. Wearing masks and carry signs, they sing a ritual chant. Deaths heads. Surgeons with blood on their whites. Cartoon children. Thirty or forty people who will never be recognized on camera. The Inspector walks to the parking lot then drives to a the precinct.

"Should you be giving an address tonight, Doctor?" As the speakers wait their turns behind the stage backdrop, the Reporter finally corners his prey. "With this morning's horror, I mean, aren't there family members you should be with now?"

"My parents and in-laws fly in later tonight. The police say there's nothing I can do to help. All other arrangements are in hand. What would you have me do? Sit in a hotel room and weep?"

Clicking off frames as he speaks, for the first time since the incident, the Reporter feels ill at ease. "I'm sorry, sir, it's only, I can only imagine what you're going through."

Another speaker leaves the waiting area and heads to the microphone. The Doctor places his hand on the Reporter's shoulder. "Don't worry. Just keep doing your job. That's what I'm doing.

"We prepared as well as we could for something like this. Only we thought it would be me. It's too much. I'll tell you straight out, I'm in a daze right now. You could drive a nail through my foot and I wouldn't feel a damn thing. Don't worry about me tonight.

But you might want to give me a thought tomorrow when the shock wears off a bit and what's happened starts kicking in."

"Do I have to eat this?" Taking his fork and spreading scrambled eggs to the far edges of his plate, the Son's whining has the Daughter rolling her eyes in despair.

"Finish up and I'll toss an extra muffin into your lunch." The Wife finds bribery, though not recommended by most child experts, works.

The Twins finish their breakfasts.

"Hurry up, both of you. The bus is here in two minutes." The Wife gathers sandwiches and buttons coats. The Son and Daughter grab books and lunch sacks.

The bus sounds its horn.

The Son runs upstairs.

"What's he doing?" The Wife wraps a scarf around her Daughter's shoulders.

"Probably forgot his homework. I'll tell them we'll be right out." Leaving books and lunch behind, the Daughter goes out the front door and signals the bus driver, who idles at the end of the walkway, to wait another minute.

"Hurry up, up there. Your sister's holding the bus for you."

"I'll be right there."

The Wife hears thumping feet above her head. "Move it. Come on."

Stepping outside the door, the Daughter signals the bus driver to hold on one more minute.

Back inside, Daughter holds a brown paper wrapped package in her hands. "Mom, this was on the porch."

Looking at her Daughter, seeing the package, the Wife immediately comprehends the situation.

"No. No. No."

Ripping through the second floor, the Explosion smashes the wire bird cage against the ceiling, sluicing the parakeet though its screen, before lifting half the roof from the house. As the Explosion seeks a way to escape the home's confines, it destroys Wife, Son and Daughter.

Alone in the basement of his home, the Third Person fiddles with mercury switches and mechanical timers, now and then glancing at television news broadcasts As the local stations show images of the rally, the Third Person divides plastic into three piles. There are two switches and one timer. The Driver. The Passenger. The Preacher. Plenty.

As the usher approaches for their offerings both the Driver and the Passenger give thanks to the Lord for allowing them to be in His service. The Driver, a baritone, and the Passenger, a tenor, join with the rest of the congregation as they sing praises to the Lord, their God.

"Killer." "Blasphemer." "Genocide." "Pederast." "Murderer." Surrounding the Preacher, demonstrators spit defamation towards the stage. Periodically the Preacher recites verses from the Old Testament, egging on those around him to higher levels of ferocity. The Preacher stands in the crowd a good thirty yards behind the masked demonstrators, who heckle speakers as they await the Doctor's appearance.

"Crowd's way too nasty, Doc. You really, really shouldn't go out there." Echoing the sentiment heard from everyone else waiting backstage, the Reporter attempts to restrain the Doctor from putting his body into what is obviously a life threatening situation.

"I have to speak." The Doctor knows he's entered a fugue state. He feels nothing. "My family's death has to mean something. We all know who killed them. They're probably in the audience right now demonstrating against us. I have to speak. The loss of my children, my wife, has to mean something. Right now the cameras are on me. It's my choice. It's what I must do."

The Reporter has nothing to say. As the Doctor is introduced, the majority of those attending the rally applaud but demonstrators surrounding the Preacher continue their invective.

The Doctor speaks through the microphone. "With my family tragedy this morning, my wife, my daughter, my son, I feel it is most important the message both my wife and myself spent our entire adult life working to spread be repeated once again."

And these are the only words the Doctor is allowed to say, for masked demonstrators have swarmed the stage, disconnecting the microphone and surrounding the Doctor. They hit him with their fists and when he falls to the stage floor, they kick him with their feet. Someone in this crowd of unidentifiable rioters pulls a knife and drives it repeatedly into the Doctor's body. The Doctor dies on the same day as the other members of his family.

"Yes, sir, we've sent all units to the scene. Thank you for calling."

At his desk, the Inspector is amazed how rapidly the calls arrive at the precinct. Most are dialing in from the stadium using their cell phones, having witnessed the execution of a human being for the first time in their lives.

The Inspector settles in for a busy night.

THE DEAL

"Shut up, Gerry. Deal the cards." Five years younger than the foursome's eldest, George is at ease intimidating the old man, even for a negligible edge.

"Simmer down. Simmer down. We're all here for one reason, a noble purpose. Gerry, let's play." Oozing with Southern sincerity, the one time engineer adds oil to roiling waters.

Scattering pasteboards about the table, the old man chuckles. "You kids don't know what it's like. I've been through all this before. Hell, only reason I got the job was because of a gathering just like this one." Gerry lifts his eyes from the green baize and smiles towards his tormenter. "George, you listen to Brother Jimmy. We're here because of our shared experience and our supposed wisdom. You bring familial emotions into this, we might have to ask you to leave."

George listens in quiet rage as Gerry calls for bets.

"You boys want another drink?" Reversing the direction of his chair, the current President moves his large frame into a more intimidating position at the table. "I'm sure one of the waiters will be more than glad to fetch a cocktail or two." With his patented smile roaring full blast and the twinkle in his eye which caused so much trouble flashing like diamonds, the Big Man puts his arm around the snarling Yalie. "George, George, George, quite the pretty pitiful mess Al and your boy got us all into. Isn't it?"

"Cracker, eat my ......" The aging Eli begins his attack when the spiritual leader from Georgia interrupts.

"Come on, fellas, we've got a load of serious work to finish tonight. And we're not getting anywhere if both of you don't put aside all your petty grievances and think about our country for a change. You with me on this, Gerry?"

"Absolutely, Jimmy. You know, George, Bill, I wasn't positive either of you should be here tonight. You two neutralize one another." The old man draws a troubled expression on his face, the same mug he used on his own boys whenever they stepped out of line. He has the experience for the job.

Putting two former opponents in their place for the moment, Gerry shifts his attention to the former Georgia Governor.

"Thanks, Gerry. Well, I think we've most of the preliminaries settled so lets..."

"Jimmy," the boy's father refuses to accept the inevitable, "Governor, why isn't our kinsman from California represented tonight? I mean, he has as much of a right to be here as we do, maybe twice as much. His views should be represented at this meeting. I'm positive Mrs. Reagan would be pleased to sit in for her husband one more time."

Not one to let a partisan blow go unanswered, the Big Dog from Arkansas adds his two cents. "I'm sure Lady Bird wouldn't mind flying in as well. Even though good old Lyndon has been in the ground a couple of years, he's probably as coherent as your old boss, George. And besides, it would be nice to hear what a real Texan has to say about how big a mess getting caught stealing an election can be. Bring on the ladies."

For a moment, the only sound heard is Connecticut dentures being ground to nothing.

"Let's stay on track, fellas," Jimmy the Conciliator takes control, "before we scheduled this meeting both sides agreed only past-Presidents and the incumbent President should be in attendance. No proxies. No spouses. We all feel badly for President Reagan but we all have to admit he has seen better times. And we can all but hope pleasant memories from his life occupy his thoughts these days."

"Amen."

"Who can hope for more?"

"Good." Carter has moderated more hostile negotiations than this, but outside his own family, he's never been involved with one which strikes so close to home. "Well, why not stop one charade right away." The peanut farmer tosses his cards into the center of the table and the others follow suit. "No more games tonight.

"Fine, fellas. Gerry and I have agreed on a few items and we would like to run them by you. See if we can arrive at something resembling unanimous agreement. For the good of the nation." Jimmy leans forward, fingers interlaced, his eyes moving between Bush Sr. and Clinton. Dealt cards lie idle before them.

"Remember, gentlemen, not one of us will leave this table completely happy." Ford nods his head in agreement. "But what I think would be appropriate right now is for the four of us to remember why we are here." Carter picks up a silver bell from the center of the table and gives the slightest shake. The bell's quiet jingle can barely be heard beyond the card table's circumference.

"You rang, sirs?"

Owing to his current rank of Vice-President, Al Gore was assigned the more prestigious job of waiter for this evening's confab. Bedecked in a cutaway tuxedo and sporting a highly starched white shirt with appropriate bow tie, strangely, Gore appears perfectly cast.

"Gore," Carter fells ill-at-ease with this evening's agreed upon salutations, "Gore, would you be good enough to serve the Presidents and myself some sandwiches. And if you might call for the bartender, I believe we will be ordering drinks as well."

"Yes, sir, Mr. President." Spinning on his heal then exiting the room, the gentleman from Tennessee remains confident that as long as he does his particular assignment more diligently than anyone else, he will be rewarded.

"What a stiff." All eyes turn toward the former Arkansas governor. "Now, now, don't you get me wrong. I dearly love and respect Al and I know in my heart and in my head he's by far the best man available for the job but, Jeez Louise..., I mean, Jimmy, Jimmy even you know what I mean. Don't you?"

Before the non-Vice-President one termer can respond, Al Gore reenters the card room and after clearing the playing cards away, sets a lazy Susan filled with sandwiches and fixings near the center of the table. "Will there be anything else, Misters President?"

Perusing the extravagant assortment of deli, none of the Presidents, not even Bush pere finds fault.

"Thanks, Al," The Big Dog recovers without a blink, "this is great. How's about our drink orders?"

"I've sent for the bartender, Mr. President, he should be with you shortly."

"Thank you, Al."

The current Vice-President backs out of the room, firmly closing the double doors behind him.

"I've always liked Gore." Gerry Ford looks toward the ceiling and rubs his chin. "Liked his folks too. They were real people."

Both Clinton and Carter catch one another's eye as Bush cuts into Ford's reminiscences.

"I liked them both too, Gerry. Too bad they weren't Republicans.

"Relax yourself, George. Where I come from, young ladies are taught to leave the dance with the young man that brought them."

Bush gives Ford the hardest of blank stares.

"President Bush, none of us here can imagine what you've been through since November's election. Not to mention the campaign and all the preparation." Ford is into his sage zen master mein. "Let's face it, with the possible exception of President Clinton here, we've all already seen our best days. You know you're getting old when you look back fondly at your youth and suddenly remember that the joyous, health filled days you're recalling occurred during your sixties. Am I right, President Carter?"

"You most certainly are, President Ford."

"So what I'm saying to you, George, is this. We know you're tired. We know how exhausting it is to captain a national election campaign. We only can imagine how mentally and physically stressful the last couple of months have been for you and your family. Not only still fighting the election war but making sure Jeb and his entire state machine don't go to jail for rigging election results down there in Florida. It's been all Jimmy and I could do just keeping President Clinton here from sending Federal troops into the Sunshine State, what a den of inequality that place is." Ford and Carter signal agreement.

"George, as a Democrat I still firmly believe the only way to get an honest vote out of the Banana Republic they call a state is to send in Federal troops. But I also know that particular action would rip this country apart. That is the only reason your son Jeb is not inside a Federal lockup right now. Gerry and I have worked harder than men our age should have to work to keep Bill here from invading Florida and taking over like Grant took Richmond. You keep all this in mind tonight."

"Massive fraud. Denial of voting rights by race. Police operating like the damn state is situated in Central America. If it weren't for Gerry and Jimmy, I'd have your whole family in a Federal pen right now, George. And you damn better well not forget it."

As the two most recent Presidents rise out of their chairs and approach one another like rutting mountain goats, Gerry Ford raises his right hand and snaps his fingers. Immediately, the potential combatants regain a portion of decorum.

"Sit down, boys. Sit. And pay attention. Among the four of us, we don't even have a full five terms. Hell, I wasn't even elected. If you think about it for a second, that's a fairly pitiful record. Of course Bill managed to get himself reelected, but, no offense, Mr. President, right now you'll probably be remembered more for your dalliances than for any accomplishments and the rest of us were shown the door as soon as the electorate had a good look. Couldn't get reelected. And we all know what that means in the history books.

"So let's do some real work tonight and maybe get this damn Union back on track." Ford nods in Carter's direction.

"Now, as I mentioned before, Gerry and I have taken care of a number of the more insignificant items. And, now, the way we divvied up this pie.

"Let's get to it. First, Al is out and Junior is in."

Clinton is on his feet. "Now hold on. there, Governor, exactly when were the results of this election decided? And by who? You and Gerry?"

Bush Senior is grinning from ear-to-ear. "Well, it's about time. That's all I have to say."

Both Carter and Ford proceed to double team the incumbent President.

"Bill, this is the only way to go."

"Son, a decision needed to be made. This country can't stand much more living in limbo."

"The Republicans are taking the White House but there will be strings attached. It is a deal like any other deal, there is something in it for both sides."

"Nobody comes out a real winner on this one."

"Where's our drinks?"

Carter puts his arm on Clinton's shoulder and leads him back to his seat. "Gerry and I cut cards for it, Bill. It was the only way to decide. We will have the Supreme Court validate our decision in the next few days. It is all over. You have to simmer down, Mr. President." Once again Carter picks up the silver bell and the Democrat candidate is in the room in a flash.

"We still need some drinks, Gore."

"I'll get him myself, Mr. President."

"Thanks, Gore."

Bush Senior makes a quick move for the door. "Well, I guess that's that, gentlemen." He places his hand on the doorknob. "I'll probably see most of you on Inauguration Day. All I have to say is, it's been one hell of a race."

Just as Bush Senior is about to exit, Ford calls him back into the room. "Not so fast, George. Nobody's leaving here until we iron out the details. Remember, nothing's final until President Carter and I say it's final. Please, return to your seat, President Bush."

Which is when the new father-of-the-President realizes he's not going to close this deal right away. He only has one goal for this meeting and he'll do whatever needs be done to achieve it. Sitting through more of this charade can't hurt much. Bush Senior parks himself back in his seat. "You go right ahead, Gerry. Take your time."

"Now we've broken it all down to a short list of both gives and takes. First off, Junior gets the four year lease. So that's one for the party of Lincoln."

"Excuse me, Mr. President," Al Gore is at the door again, "I'm sorry but none of the staff can locate the bartender. If it's all right with you gentlemen, I'll take your drink orders in his place."

All eyes turn toward Bush Senior, who, after a moment's hesitation, places his order, "I'm sorry, Gore, scotch-on-the-rocks with a twist, if you would be so kind."

"Anybody know where the bartender's gotten off to, Al?" As he speaks, Clinton uses a two finger hand signal indicating his usual.

"Not behavior we expect around here, do we, President Carter?"

"Not at all, President Ford. Mr. President Ford, those judicial appointments we were discussing?"

"Yes, President Carter?"

"One moment, Gerry. Gore, I'll have a cranberry juice with lime. President Ford?"

"Yes, yes, sorry to keep you waiting, Mr. Vice-President. Bourbon and branch will be fine with me. Lyndon certainly knew how to drink, didn't he?"

"Thank you, Misters President." And Al Gore again backs out of the room.

"Judicial appointments?" Clinton cocks his head to one side and stares at the two former chief executives running the meeting.

"One of the negotiating points. Gerry and I were stuck on particular bone of contention one for a few hours yesterday. Now that the bartender seems to have gone AWOL again, that settles that."

Almost apologetically, George H. W. Bush asks, "None at all?"

"I tried as hard as I could, George, but the four of us are sitting here eating sandwiches with nothing to drink." Ford shakes his head in resignation. "We can't give the boy power like that. Not if we're all going to agree on this."

"Presidents Ford, Carter," Clinton leans forward in his seat, "I think it's about time you let President Bush and myself in on exactly what kind of deal you've negotiated. We already know who won the big prize. Let's get down with the devil and hear the details."

Bush nods and Ford looks to Carter who flips sheets in his notebook as he speaks. "Since President Ford and I immediately realized we would be the deciding votes in all of this, we took it upon ourselves to work out an agreement which seemed as fair and as workable as anyone could expect. You might want to object here and there but if you would hold off on those objections until after I read all we have worked out so far, both Gerry and I would appreciate that very much."

Bush and Clinton nod in agreement.

"Fine. Item one: Bush Junior is declared the official winner by the Supreme Court.

"We had to chose one of them so Gerry and I cut cards for it. Gerry won.

"Now to make this deal as fair as possible, here are the gives and takes.

"One: Junior only gets the one term. He can run again if he wants, but he will not be reelected.

"Two: there will be no Congressional hearings of any significance regarding this year's debacle in the State of Florida.

"Three: Al Gore does not run for election in 2004.

"Four: There will be an amnesty declared, if necessary, for Jeb Bush and his entire political machine. Neither party will raise a serious objection should this come about.

"Five: all classified records from both the Reagan and Bush Senior administration will remain under seal until death of the principals.

"Six: no Federal troops will be sent to the State of Florida.

"Seven: Gerry and I only recently agreed upon this one. Junior will not be allowed to appoint any new Justices to the Supreme Court." Carter places his notebook on the table and leans back in his chair.

"Jimmy, Governor Carter, that's it?" Clinton's anger is impossible to disguise. "We let them steal the White House, no Congressional hearings, no prosecutions, and all we get is an empty promise about frat boy being a one term president?" Clinton glares at Carter like Caesar at Brutus.

"Best deal to be made, Bill. Now is the time to cut our losses and move on to the next battle."

"I'm ordering in Federal troops." The President of the United States again lifts himself from his chair, rises to full height and begins to leave the room.

"Stop, Mr. President." Gerry Ford raises his hand in the universal halt signal. "You know as well as the rest of us that we can't allow you to send troops into Florida. The risk of another Civil War is too great."

The current President now faces three former Presidents who, united as one, do have enough political clout to keep Clinton from exercising his power as Chief Executive.

"You boys forcing me to swallow this? And like it? Jimmy, is this the very best we can possibly do?"

"Bill, they stole the election. Under your watch, you best remember that as well. There is plenty enough blame to go around."

Backing through the double doors, Al Gore carries in a tray of drinks which he distributes around the table. "Everyone all set here?" Met with grunts and silence, the waiter of the evening exits quietly.

"Now, I suppose you all are going to make me tell Al as well? Jeez Louise, fellas, why don't you up and rip me a new one while you're at it?"

"Jimmy and I will inform the Vice-President, Mr. President. George, you'll tell your son, if he ever shows up."

"Right, President Ford."

"Well, I guess that about wraps it all up. Oh, yeah, if a Supreme Court Justice ups and dies, Jimmy and I will decide on the replacement. Bill and Bob Dole will be our seconds if it comes to that. Well, I'm tired. Goodnight, guys."

Putting aside his momentary fit of pique, Clinton reaches out to shake Ford's hand. "Thank you, Mr. President. I guess every thirty years or so you get to do one of these emergency interventions. Nice job."

"Thank you, Mr. President."

And as the four men shake hands and prepare to leave, the

double doors swing open to reveal the slightly befuddled, moderately unkempt, bartender for the evening.

"Gosh, I'm sorry I got here so late. You see my usual driver has the night off and wouldn't you know it, we got caught behind some kind of an accident which slowed us down for I don't know how long and then the new guy behind the wheel, must be from Central America or some country like that, couldn't understand any of the directions I was giving him and we ended up somewhere near the airport and it was only then I was able to get my bearings and figure out how to get here. So I'm so sorry I'm so late but I'll guarantee to all you right now you can be darn sure it's never going to happen again."

All four colleagues now speak as one.

"Oh, crap."

RAPTURE

Alicia is seated on the opposite side of the room when Omar lowers his eyes to read the newspaper headline. As he focuses her way again, she is gone.

Omar is all by himself.

Moving from his desk, he walks across the office and stares through bulletproof windows. For the first time since Omar's installation, he studies the garden. He considers the clarity of a single rose.

Quiet. Since the two hundred employees who daily inhabit this building vacated the premises, Omar is no longer surrounded by human harmonics; snorts, heavy breathing, creaking bones, rustle of clothes. It's as if noon became four in the morning. But even then there would be people, in offices, guards, telephone operators, janitors, folks like that. All gone now.

One rose. Omar focuses on one rose among many.

EARLIER

During the State dinner, alarms sound as ambassadors and heads of state disappear into the ether. Omar's security detail freezes in place, not knowing the threat's origin. By dessert the staff has vanished.

A serenity descends as Omar and his wife, Alicia, return to the official residence.

"The Lord is in His glory." The First Lady smiles at her husband. Her face radiates elation from a job well done.

"I am but an instrument of His divine will. Any grace flowing through me is His alone. I am but one small part in His all knowing plan. Would you enjoy a martini, Alicia?"

"Omar, you haven't had a drink in years. Why now?"

"I believe our Lord and Savior won't mind if we indulge in a small one. After all, we won't be around long enough to get drunk. I've been a good boy, haven't I, Mommy?"

"You certainly have, Omar. Both of us have been very good. That's why the Lord will take us to his bosom. You know that, don't you, Poppy?"

"I prayed, Mommy, I prayed. I prayed, 'Dear Jesus, when You come to take all the God fearing, family loving Christians to Your eternal breast, take Mommy and me last. Take us at the end so we may carry on Your work until the very, very last instant. Thank You, Lord.'" Omar serves his wife her martini, two olives, ultra dry. It's been years since he poured his last martini, but he retains the knack.

"Poppy, could you ever have imagined we'd travel so far on our spiritual quest? Here we are, the Rapture surrounds us, and we're having a quiet toast to our Lord and Personal Savior. We've lived a good life, haven't we, Poppy?"

"Yes, we have, Mommy. And we've done the Lord's work. We've followed Our Savior's instructions. The final battle will soon begin. Wonder if we'll see any of it, Mommy." Omar savors the first drink he's had, in what? It must be two years since the last relapse.

"Omar, we'll see as much as Our Good Lord wishes us to see, no more, no less. Did you watch the way Our Savior took the Reverend Grallway tonight? The Rapture is pretty unbelievable even when it's happening right in front of us."

"Poof! and he's gone, Mommy. Poof! Poof! Poof! Have another?" After not touching a real drink for such a long time, Omar notices its effects immediately. Thank goodness he stocked the bar last week. "Poof! Poof! Poof!"

Alicia nods. "There Grallway was, in the middle of his blessing. He'd been speaking, for what, five minutes? That man was barely warming up. He's delayed my dinner more times than I want to remember. Thank you very much. I recall one perfectly good piece of roast beef that was so stone cold by the time he finished his benediction, I couldn't eat a single bite. Even for a man of the cloth, he certainly enjoys hearing himself speak."

"Careful now, Mommy, we'll be seeing the good Reverend soon enough. Poof! We'll be with him, standing on the right hand of Our Lord. Cheese crackers?"

Omar and Alicia savor their much delayed cocktails.

"There was the time....."

"Not now, Omar. Enjoy the quiet. Praise the Lord and pass the cocktail napkins."

"Mommy, you shouldn't kid Our Lord like that. Even though he's my Personal Savior, he might take that too personal."

"Tee hee."

"Seriously, sugar dumpling, is everyone supposed to be Raptured already? I thought enough folks would be left out of the Rapture so there'd be a real bang-up Armageddon battle. I guess we're going to miss that too. Dang Rapture."

"I wouldn't be so sure, Poppy. Maybe everyone wasn't taken to stand next to Our Lord. Maybe it was only the good folks who work for us. Poppy, you know only good Christians are allowed near us."

"You think so?"

"Oh, yes. All employees are screened. They've gone to the Lord. Atheists, liberals, and Democrats can't come anywhere near us. I'm sure there will be plenty of Jesus haters left to die in flames and blood when Armageddon arrives."

"Not our kind of people at all."

"Some even call themselves Christians, Poppy, but, really, they aren't." Alicia turns on a television. Scanning the channels, it's all static. "Seems the important network people were true Christians as well."

"After we moved here, all essential positions in major industries were taken over by certified Christians, Mommy. And those same folks are now standing at Our Lord's right hand. Christian leaders are right now sitting down to pre-dinner cocktails with Our Lord and Savior Jesus Christ. It's just you and me left, Mommy. We're the only real Christians left in the world. We're left to do Our Savior's work." Omar tilts his glass to his wife. "Here, it's like the headline in the newspaper." As Omar reaches down for yesterday's Washington Times, Alicia becomes one with the cosmos.

"Mommy? Are you with Jesus, Mommy?" Omar looks at his wife's drink, at the indentation in the cushion where she'd been sitting. "Mommy, did you go to Our Savior?"

"Poof?" Omar looks around the room for his wife.

"Poof!" Omar strokes his jaw in amazement.

"Poof."

He paces the circumference of the office. "Lord, I know You've taken them all to be at Your side. I know You're ready to launch Armageddon. Please, Lord, let me be of some last service to You."

Omar falls to his knees.

"You know I'm on Your side, Jesus. You know everything we've done, we've done in Your name. We followed Your prophecies. We obeyed Your commandments. We brought Christianity back to the Middle East, back to the Holy Land. We smote heathens and idolaters. We made this great nation Christian once again.

"But I will do even more, Lord. I will listen for Your instructions." Omar stands up and out of habit brushes dust from the knees of his slacks.

Odd not having Mommy around. Mommy was with him such a long time. Alicia saw Omar through all his trials. She'd picked him out of the gutter and taken him to the most important office imaginable. All with the Lord's help, of course.

"Maybe it's time for me now, Lord." Omar polishes off his drink and raises both his arms into the air. "It's time, Jesus. Take Your servant to Your bosom."

Omar stands in his office with arms raised to the Lord.

And he waits.

And he waits.

And he waits.

After half an hour, Omar lowers his arms and returns to his desk.

Omar drums his fingers on the blotter. He inserts a disc into his stereo but when the machine powers up, all he hears is static. Must be something in the air.

Moving across the room the President snags a gin bottle from the wetbar. "Guess it's you and me again, old friend." Pouring another martini, Omar plops into the chair most recently occupied by his wife. "Mommy, I'm coming to you. Don't you worry yourself. I'll be standing with you real soon."

Fifteen minutes later, Omar treats himself to a refill.

After two more martinis, Omar feels the need to reconnoiter the situation. He fumbles with the lock on his office door. He stumbles into the outer office, then outside into fresh air.

Silence. Nothing. Where yesterday would have been the muffled roar of twenty-four hour a day traffic, now he hears nothing. Guards who man security stations on the driveway are no longer there. No cars, slowly cruise with drivers rubbernecking the residence, hoping to glimpse the Number One man.

Even Omar, never swift to grasp the obvious, knows what's going on. Further exploration will be as useless as this short, sodden sortie.

"Jesus, it's time for me. Don't You think? I mean, jeez, what do You want me to do? I mean, tell me, Lord."

Omar parks himself on the residence's front door steps. Gin bottle in left hand, martini glass in right, Omar inspects the righteous world only a bareknuckle drunk can imagine.

EARLIER

"Breaker. Breaker. Bombs away, bubbalah." Omar looks up and down the War Room's conference table. "Come on, boys, say the sacred words and let's get this show on the road."

Fifteen senior officers focus on their Commander-in-Chief. The Chairman of the Joint Chiefs addresses his subordinates, "'Brightsky 697' is a go. I repeat 'Brightsky 697' is a go."

And those syllables began the final war. The war to end all wars. The war which ends known life on earth. Peace at last, peace at last, with no people left, peace at last.

Omar gave the order he was destined to give. As Commander-in-Chief of the most powerful country on Earth, only he can unleash these ultimate dogs of war. Within seconds of issuing his command, already airborne bombers follow carefully honed battle plans. Robot bombs vaporize the first homes in prelude to the

Rapture.

"Bombs away. Ten-four. Over and out." Omar doesn't know if he's saying these words aloud or running them through his mind like a nonsense mantra. Breaker. Breaker. Bombs away, bubbalah. I'm a little teapot, short and stout. Here is my handle. Breaker. Breaker. Bombs away and one hundred thousand little dark people are taken from this veil of tears and sent air express to Our Savior. He'll judge you. You're not Christians, but if you led good lives, you won't be punished. You won't be sitting on the right hand of Our Lord and Savior, but it'll be a better life than what you're living now. Bombs away! Ten-four, over and out.

Poof!

Boom!

Bombs away!

When Omar discovered he'd been appointed President, it was as much a shock to him as it was to the majority of voters who'd cast ballots. Here he was, this 50 something ex-lush who'd never accomplished anything in his life, and somehow his Daddy finagled him the world's most important job. His family had been in the ruling oligarchy for generations. Hell, one of Omar's ancestors invaded South America all by himself, but for a father to steal his son the Presidency, how great a dad is that? Sure made up for missed Little League games.

"Mr. President, the enemy is engaging in little or no resistance. Advance troops should enter the capital within the hour."

"Good job, General." Generals really enjoy being complimented. They mostly rise to their elevated rank by sucking up to superiors throughout their careers. Now, since they've achieved high enough rank so to sit in the same room as the President of the United States, they've run out of folks in positions to toss them a dog biscuit, pat them on their shaved little heads, and tell them what good puppies they are. No matter how much they despise Omar for his lack of ability, Omar forces himself to compliment the Generals. He restrains himself from carrying General Treats in his pockets.

After Omar's appointment, his dad and the rest of the political team agreed the best way to make sure Omar, four years hence, actually got elected, or re-elected, the preferred lie, was to have the boy become a War President.

"Omar."

"Yes, Dad."

"Omar, you're a good son. I want you to know that."

"I know that. You're a great pops too."

"Omar, me and the fellas have been strategizing and we've some bad news for you."

"Yes?"

"Son, you've never been to war. In the job you've got now, you'll need to kill some folks. You know that, don't you, boy?"

"Sure, Dad, but they won't be our folks. Right?"

"We've found you a nice, easy place to invade. You know where I mean."

"Sure."

"When I was doing this job, they pulled me back from total victory and I suffered for it. I wanted that country bad, but I didn't have the steel for it. So I lost my re-election bid. I wanted to be a War President, but they pulled me away. I paid. Now you can make things right."

"Dad?"

"Listen, boy, you fried some scum as governor, but this is different. You're going to firebomb women and children. You got the stomach for it?"

"Sure, Dad." Omar barely manages to stay awake.

The old man isn't sure he's gotten through to the boy. Omar knows what his father is talking about. The boy also knows his actions will bring on the Rapture.

"Son, I'm talking big time slaughter here. We need mass murder, at least, if we're going to really get you elected this time around."

"Sure, Dad." Omar keeps his thoughts to himself. The Lord will call you to sit at His right hand when the Rapture arrives. He can't tell his father this. His father is to be revered for his good works but Omar's dad isn't a true believer. The son shall tend to the father's needs.

So war plans are formulated and father and son for the first time work as a team. His dad bent his formidable mind to the details of a multi-theater military campaign, scheduled to crescendo at the precise moment necessary to amass the majority of votes needed for a legitimate second term.

But Omar's mind is never fully occupied planning these future wars. There won't be a second election, but his father doesn't need to know this.

"Mr. President, the Second Division is now entering the city. Resistance remains minimal."

Which is about the way Omar was advised it would happen by

Reverend Grallway, the only advisor Omar really needs.

"Omar, the Rapture will arrive only after you've conquered the non-believers. Their leader must fall to your sword." Grallway had counseled the high and mighty for years. It helped he conversed with Our Lord and Savior Jesus Christ each and every morning and evening.

"My actual sword, Reverend."

"Your metaphorical sword should suffice, Mr. President. Do you speak with your Personal Lord and Savior every day?" Grallway eases himself into a chair facing the Commander in Chief.

"Certainly, Reverend. I speak to Him and He speaks to me. Sometimes He speaks to both Alicia and myself at the same time."

"He converses with both of you at the same time?" Good Reverend Grallway has heard most of the choice ones before, but this is new. "You mean he uses the same words?"

"Sure, Reverend. Alicia and I share direct communication with Our Personal Lord and Savior."

"Tell me more."

"Mommy and me pray together morning and night. You know that. Right, Reverend?"

"Of course."

"Well, when we pray, after we speak privately with Our Personal Lord and Savior for a few minutes, Mommy tells me what the Lord is saying to her."

"And what does Jesus say to you?" Reverend Grallway adjusts the balance of his buttocks.

"Very odd first time it happened. Just as Mommy begins

telling Jesus's words to me, I'm minding Mommy's words, and suddenly my Personal Lord and Savior is saying exactly the same thing to me. I'm listening to Mommy with my ears and I'm hearing Jesus Christ through my mind, my heart and my soul. Pretty amazing if I say so myself."

"Certainly is, Mr. President. Mr. President, if you don't mind my asking, if I'm not intruding on any covenant between you and your Lord, do you mind my asking what it is Jesus has been saying to you lately? I don't mean to pry, but as your spiritual counselor, it would be useful for me to know."

"Of course, Reverend Grallway, of course. I understand completely."

"But we are talking about the words of Our Lord and Savior Jesus Christ here, and His true word must be spread to all His faithful children."

"Certainly. Reverend, Alicia and I have spoken about this same subject many times. We both feel we should bear witness to the everlasting truths of Our Lord Jesus Christ. But...."

"Omar, Mr. President, how can there be any "buts" when it comes to spreading the joyous Word?" Reverend Granville switches weight to his other cheek. "We must all bear witness."

"I agree, Reverend. But there are considerations I need take into account."

"Does Jesus speak to you on matters of National Security?"

"Absolutely. One hundred percent. Jesus is looking out for this country better than I ever could. That's a fact."

"And what does He say to you and the First Lady, Mr. President?"

Omar ponders the question for a moment then decides it's best to share. "Bomb them. Bomb every living one of them. Bomb them until they scream for mercy."

"Bomb who, Mr. President?"

"Bomb the heathens, Reverend. Bomb them until they're willing to accept Jesus Christ as their Personal Savior and Lord. Bomb them until we bring on the Rapture when all good Christians will be taken up to sit at the right hand of Our Lord Jesus Christ. Bomb them until Armageddon, when forces of light forever dispel the forces of darkness and sinners and fornicators and idolaters will be tossed into the fiery pit where rats eat their flesh and they scream for Jesus' mercy until the end of time. Care for a mint, Reverend Grallway?"

The good Reverend perches on the edge of his seat. "No thank you, Mr. President. I'm watching my weight. Mr. President, are you saying Our Lord commanded you to bring about Armageddon?"

"Well, yes, Reverend. That's what I've been saying."

"And Our Lord repeated this to Alicia at the same time?

"Exactly."

"And that's why we launched our attacks?"

"Absolutely."

"And that's why you started this war?"

"What's more important than performing Our Lord and Savior Jesus Christ's work?"

EARLIER

"Mr. President? Mr. President, we've taken the executive palace."

Omar awakens from a dream of summer evening softball. Gentle breezes caress Omar's face as he winds up, then pitches the ball, slowly and underhand. As the batter swings and connects, the softball shatters into thousands of glass and metal shards which rocket back into the infield and beyond, impaling his teammates who fall to the ground. Continuing their flight, these deadly darts penetrate the outfield and carry into the bleachers, mowing down row after row of docile fans.

Omar remains untouched by the projectiles firing past him. The team's manager emerges from the dugout and makes his way to the pitcher's mound. Taking thousand dollar bills from his hip pocket, the manager counts out crumpled notes into Omar's outstretched hand.

"Mr. President, we have initial casualty estimates from the air campaign."

Now is the time. Omar's dad had warned him. His military advisors tried to prepare their commander for the awesome responsibility, thousands of innocent war victims' blood on his hands. Screaming children enveloped in flames. Friendly combatants dying or grossly mutilated. "Initial casualty estimates", are this morning's box scores.

"Thank you, General."

Solid, heavy bond paper. Omar likes his reports printed on stationary weighty enough to support the information they contain.

Thirty-five thousand estimated dead in first wave of aerial bombings.

Omar absorbs the numbers. Thirty-five thousand dead human beings he'd never met and never would. Thirty-five thousand less non-Christians. Thirty-five thousand people closer to bringing on the Rapture.

Omar leaves the War Room and returns to the Private Residence.

"Alicia, do you know where my putter is?" Hearing no response, Omar searches his private closets. Eventually he finds his favorite offset putter. Grabbing two golf balls from a dresser drawer, Omar heads into the family room, tosses down his electronic ball return, and pretends he's on the golf course.

After sinking two six footers in a row, Omar speaks to his Personal Lord and Savior, "Jesus, I've sent thousands to You today and I just want to say, I hope You realize what a good job I'm doing for You down here." Omar misses his next two putts and is forced to retrieve them himself. The putting machine he's using only fires back balls if his putts hit the machine. Omar's last shots were way off mark.

"Jesus, I don't know if You know, but I think You've got the best guy for the job doing the job right now. And that's me. Folks like my Daddy, he's a great man let me tell You, but folks like my Daddy, well, they don't have the, clear, vision I have. And a person needs, clear, vision to do Your work.

"Just the other day my Daddy told me I'd be sick to my stomach when the casualty reports arrived. He said he lost his lunch when they reported how many died first time he sent in troops. But that's him. He's a great man but he isn't, gifted, with my, clear, vision." Omar sinks one and misses another. So he plays with one ball until forced to retrieve them both.

"Jesus, when I saw thirty-thousand, or something like that, dead, You know how I felt? I'm sure You do but let me tell You all the same, so You know that I know. Jesus, I felt good. Thirty-thousand dead, so far, and while we chin wag even more heading to, eternal, damnation. Jesus, I felt great! Probably a hundred thousand heading Your way before the end of today. All in praise of You, Lord Jesus. All in praise to You.

"Jesus, I'll have my followers swim in, heathen, blood. They'll swim in blood up to their necks to fulfill Your eternal prophecy. Help me kill them in Your honor, Lord Jesus. I praise Your Name and I'll send all enemies of true Christianity to, eternal, damnation, quick as a minute.

"Praise be to You, Lord."

Omar misses two putts in a row.

EARLIER

"Dah dah de dah dah de dah de dah de dah dah. Dah dah de dah de de dah de de dah dah."

"Hum it again, Mommy. I want to you to hum it again." Omar, face flush with satisfaction, nudges his wife's shoulder. "Come on, Mommy, it's been weeks." Omar snuggles close as they lay in their bed.

Alicia marks the page in her book then stares at her husband.

"I don't know what you're so happy about. Daddy arranged all this. You didn't do a damn thing worth mentioning."

"I know, Mommy, but, please? I'm really, really too excited to sleep right now."

"Alright. But turn off the lights."

As bedside lamps are extinguished and the room goes black, Omar feels his wife's hand roughly grab his penis and as the rhythmic stroking begins she hums and hails the Chief once again. "Dah dah de dah dah de dah de dah de dah dah. Dah dah de dah de de dah de de dah dah."

EARLIER

"Congratulations, son, I knew you'd make it when you put your mind to it."

"Thanks, Dad. I wouldn't have made it without you. And Our Lord Jesus Christ, of course."

"Damn straight you couldn't have. Glad to help. Son, you want to lay off the "Jesus" stuff, with the public. We've got a coalition going here, and not all our supporters are good Christians like you and me."

"You're kidding me, aren't you?" Omar has never heard this before.

"No, son, we've got Catholics and Jews, Moslems, and even some Buddhists. Whatever silly religions you can think of, we've got backers. Whoever they are, these folks know the value of a dollar."

"But they'll never sit on the right hand of Our Lord."

"Omar, your mother and I were delighted you finding religion so late in life. You'd been lost in that wilderness of drugs and alcohol for so many years, we knew any change would be an improvement, but, trust me on this one, son, lay off the holy rollerisms in public. A little "In God We Trust" and "God Bless America" is alright. But, as a rule, and having done this job myself, keep your religion private and life will be easier for you and everybody else."

"Yes, sir."

After many government officials are paid off, promised better positions or, like the Supreme Court, given everything they want, including powerful jobs for their extended families, Omar takes the oath.

"Thank You, Jesus, thank You for having those Jewish folks not be able to read their ballots. And thanks again for all those votes appearing out of nowhere like manna. A miracle. Thank You, Lord."

Putting his hand on the Bible, Omar swears an oath to the people while promising his Lord and Personal Savior to bring their world to an end.

"Omar, congratulations, I know the good wishes of all true Christian Americans are with you tonight." Reverend Granville corners Omar at a post-Inaugural gala. "I know you'll do your best promoting Our Lord's work in the President's office." Granville is a consulting vice-president for the conglomerate hosting this soiree.

"Reverend, let me tell you one thing, and it ain't two, when the good people of this country appointed me President, they got a two-for-one surprise. They got me as their President, and Our Lord and Savior, Jesus, Christ as my Chief of Staff, Secretary of State, and Attorney General. This country will be, Christian, once again."

Hail! Hail! The Chief's all here!

Dah dah de dah dah de dah de dah de dah dah. Dah dah de dah de de dah de de dah dah.

And as the two leaders shake hands, the Marine Band plays Omar's new theme song in the adjoining ballroom. Preacher and President rejoin their wives, and the four move next door where they present themselves as a cohesive unit.

Arriving at the dais, Alicia stands next to her husband but as he clears his throat to speak, she retreats a step.

From out of nowhere, a voice, "Ladies and Gentlemen, the President of the United States of America and ...." The crowd's roar drowns out what else the announcer has to say. Omar raises his hands high above his head and waves to the adoring throng. For two minutes, friends and supporters maintain thunderous applause until Omar silences them with a gesture. The new President of the United States of America taps the microphone once. He addresses his fellow countrymen.

"Praise Jesus! God bless America!"

Again the ballroom is overwhelmed by extended applause and supportive howls.

"Thank-You, Jesus. And thanks to you all for being here tonight, sharing this, great, victory!

"I want to tell all you folks about a vision I had for this, great, country's future. A vision for our whole, entire planet. With the help of you, good, people, we're going to bring Our Lord's vision into being."

EARLIER

"These do, Governor?" One day a week, that's all Omar is allowed for himself. One day a week, Saturday night, if nothing important is scheduled. One day he can be himself, not their marionette.

"Yeah, fine. Now get the hell out of here."

"Yes, Governor." As his servant closes the door, Omar hears the dead bolt slip into place.

"Fuck your mother, you son-of-a-bitch." The Governor slumps into the couch.

Six days a week Omar works from sunup to sundown. One night a week is Omar's alone. He can do what he wants. As long as he stays out of sight, locked in this hotel suite.

Security brings him whatever he wants. Right now, laid out on a low coffee table are six lines of coke, an unopened fifth of Jack Daniels, and three empty Coors cans. Anyway, the night's young.

Last weekend they brought in twins. Brunettes. Mid-twenties. Surgery to pretty them up. Partied until morning when Omar went to church with the family. In church Omar remained as high as the night before, constantly replaying the previous evening's menage with those two silicon enhanced twins and more nose candy than he's seen in years.

But that was last week. Tonight should be even more fun.

Omar picks up the plastic straw and as quick as you can say Jack Daniels, two lines of coke disappear.

Poof!

Poof!

Four left. Where's the babes? Omar requested the same hospitality selection this weekend as last. Yowie! Zowie! He cracks open the Jack bottle and inhales a sweet shot.

Sucking down a Coors, Omar inspects the coke vials. Three grams should last the night. If they run out, he'll order more from Security.

"I'm the fucking Governor, chump. You do what I say and everything will be peachy." Omar isn't perfectly sure but he's pretty sure he's just snorted some damn fine coke. "Damn right it is. I'm Governor. Only the best for Governor." Now Omar is raging. In the blink of an eye, two more lines disappear.

"Bring on the bitches! Bring 'em to Big Omar. Governor Big Omar. Bring 'em on." Now Omar's used to doing more than his fair share of cocaine but something doesn't feel right this evening.

"Damn right, something's not right. Security! God damn, get your ass in here. Security!"

Omar sits down. He fumbles at his wrist, groping for a pulse. His throat and nasal passages feel on fire. A neck vein throbs like it's about to pop. For lack of anything smarter to do, Omar pours himself another shot of Jack, then, putting the shot glass to his nose, he snorts most of the liquor out of the glass and into his nostrils as if Jack Daniels were China white.

"Security!" Omar's screams his lungs out but the door remains shut.

Raising himself to full height, for a moment Omar remembers last weekend and the twins. Falling, he finds himself on the suite's floor, his tongue licking raspy fibers of wall-to-wall carpeting.

"Bring it on, you bastards. I'll clean your clocks."

Right before Omar passes out, he grabs the bourbon bottle. One more for the road.

"Wake up, Governor."

Omar, flat on his back, staring at the ceiling, hears words but doesn't react. He has no idea where he is or who's talking.

"Come on, sugar. Wake up now."

That voice he knows. Alicia. Must be home in bed. But why doesn't Omar recognize this ceiling?

"Wake up, Governor. We're here to help."

"Wake up, son. Time to get some work done. That means you, boy."

Mom? Must be you, Mom. Who else? Alicia, Mom.

"Wake up now, Governor."

Reverend Granville? Jeez, what the hell is going on?

Turning his head to the right, Omar tries to move his body. No way. Arms and his legs are shackled to bed posts. Omar lies spreadeagled, naked and bound. Did the twins do this to him?

"Governor, you overdosed on drugs. Can you hear me?" Granville's voice shrieks into Omar's head like a dawn trolley car's rusty wheels.

Omar nods.

"Son, you've been heading down this same bad road for years. We're here to set you back on the right course."

Spreadeagled, handcuffed, and bare assed in front of his

mother and minister. Omar wants to say a few words in his own defense but his efforts prove useless.

Alicia, Mom and the Reverend berate him in shifts. For the first half hour Reverend Granville spouts fire and brimstone.

After the Reverend finishes, Omar's mother takes command of the lash.

Disgrace to the family.

Waste of talent.

Squandered opportunities.

Omar's heard it before. This isn't his first intervention. Where do the twins come into all this?

And then sweet wife, Alicia, takes over.

For most of his life the only woman who truly scared Omar was his mother. Then he met Alicia.

Alicia sits on the corner of the bed, and before uttering word one, extracts a six inch long wooden handled steak knife from the oversized alligator handbag she carries all the time.

"Omar, you know I have to cut you again? Don't you?"

EARLIER

She's always there.

When he brought women back to the apartment, it only took Alicia a word or two with Omar's playmates to have his latest trophies click clacketing their high heels down the stairs and out the door.

Alicia was always there. She'd fix him coffee, or clean him up, or put him to bed, or join him in bed. She'd do whatever necessary.

Omar's and Alicia's was an arranged marriage, a tradition in both clans. Omar's mother introduced the two during one of his dad's campaigns. Later, after extended discussions with his father, the son realized keeping Alicia around was in his best interest.

Come the Spring, with Granville performing the ceremony, Alicia and Omar set up housekeeping as proper newlyweds. For the most part Alicia kept out of Omar's way. After a couple of years, kids cemented the original deal. Everybody seemed happy. Omar's lifestyle didn't change much, five, six days a week, partying, coke, golf and women. Sundays, family and politics.

Then Alicia put her foot down.

Omar's first intervention set the pattern for those following. After he'd fallen off a barstool and bruised his face, Alicia threw in the towel. Only when Omar screwed up in a manner easily observed by the public did interventions occur. One day he'd learn.

That night he passed out in the living room and when he awoke, he was tied to a chair in the guest bedroom.

Reverend Granville did a half hour.

Omar's mother screamed at him for thirty minutes.

Neither pierced Omar's drug haze.

Then Alicia took a shift. Alone with her husband, Alicia explained how she wasn't a child any longer and how Omar certainly wasn't anybody's idea of an ideal husband.

Omar tried to negotiate with his bride but being strapped to a chair and slurring one's words never help a fella's argument.

Alicia said how she'd been wild when she was young and how her running around spoiled her chances of finding a husband worth having.

Mostly what Omar was hearing from his wife was blah, blah, blah, de la blah, blah, blah. When she took that steak knife from her damned handbag, Omar began paying attention.

Alicia explains how she and her then boyfriend became involved with people with whom they shouldn't have become involved. She explains how her then boyfriend, the love of her life, the one man she'd die for, not only cheated on her with other women, in public, but also stole from her and bragged about it, in public.

Alicia elaborated in gruesome detail how she accidentally backed over her former boyfriend with a borrowed pickup truck. How she accidentally backed over her dead boyfriend's body two more times, and while accidentally backing over her dead boyfriend's body for the fourth time, she stopped the truck, stepped outside the cab, and checked to make sure her front right tire rested on her boyfriend's collapsed chest.

Alicia tells how she loves her dead boyfriend more than she could ever love anyone again for as long as she lives.

"You get my drift, sugar?"

EARLIER

Fairy lights twinkle around the leaves. Stay behind the bushes. Keep low to the ground. Nobody will see you. Crawl to the next shrub. Careful. Don't let curious eyes find you. They're after me. They're all around. Have to hide or they'll flush me out. Stay away from the light. The light will let them know where you are. Hide behind the hedges. Watch the Fairies dance on the leaves.

Omar's been sipping heavy for eight weeks. For the past four days he hasn't slept at all. In this town almost a week and he's running out of cash. Omar stopped using his credit cards two weeks back when he realized how easily his parents could track him down. He'd withdrawn ten thousand dollars from the accounts and he's almost through it.

Omar crouches behind a hedge surrounding an office building. You'd have to look very, very hard to see him.

You better watch out.

Must move. There.

Omar darts from the hedge's shelter to another bush he doesn't recognize but serves his purpose. The Fairies dance on this tree's leaves as they do on all the others.

Talk to me, little ones. Have I crossed over to your world?

This is a world few see. If only people were aware. But some know it exists. That's why Omar avoids the light.

You better not cry.

Omar knows they've been after him for months. During the day he stays locked in his motel room with shades pulled down tight. If the sunlight touches him, he knows they'll find out where he is. Any light will give him away. He must stay out of the light. Avoid the light. This must be why they persecute vampires.

He sees you when you're sleeping.

Omar feels his heart beat. Faster. Faster. They'll try to kill him next. They try to kill all men in his family. But they won't get Omar. They'll never find Omar. Omar will hide in the wilderness at night and escape the Sun during the day.

A light flashes through Omar's camouflage foliage and he flattens himself against the wall. Another car passes down the street.

He knows if you've been bad or good.

Omar could fuck a wall right now but it wouldn't help. He must hold it all in. They want his sperm. If he gives up his sperm it will be the end of the world. Omar hasn't gotten laid or jerked off in eight weeks. He'll die if that happens.

I'm telling you why.

Stay out of the light. Hide. They don't want you around. You're not like they are. Loser. Even your baby brother does better than you. Weakling.

I'll show them. I'll show all of them.

You keep drinking, boy. And you best stay out of our way.

So be good for goodness sake.

Listen, Omar. They know what they're talking about.

The Fairies. Omar finally hears the words the Fairies speak. Streetlight illuminates the leaves, showing Fairyland for those with will and concentration.

Listen to them, Omar. You can be great if you listen to them and follow in the footsteps of those who've gone before you.

Omar gazes into Fairyland.

Fairyland, Omar, bring the people to Fairyland.

"Yes. Yes. I'll bring the world to Fairyland." Omar rises to his full height. "I'll make my parents proud. I'll bring everyone to Fairyland. The worlds will no longer be separate. This will be my gift."

And with noble ambitions prodding him, Omar emerges from his hiding place and proudly steps into the street. Into the light.

Omar will save all humankind.

Santa Claus is coming to town!

Fairyland!

Rapture!

KABOOM!

DO NOT READ THE FOLLOWING TWO STORIES

HOMAGE TO A GREAT BROAD

J eremy walks. When he goes to the store, he speaks with the people working. He makes small jokes and gives them to the people who take his money. Jeremy believes it is always easy to make people laugh when you are giving them money. He then walks away and looks at the other people on the street who are looking at the other people on the street. The street is a fine place to see people. Jeremy feels himself lucky he does not often meet people on the street he knows. He often meets people on the street but he does not know them. It is rare that he knows someone he meets on the street. He does not mind meeting someone he knows on the street but very often he does not want to meet on the street someone he had met on the street.

If Jeremy has a problem, the problem is he has inclination to take things. As an inclination it is not very large. He has much larger inclinations. His inclination to stay warm is also large but it is not as large as his inclination to eat. Jeremy has many inclinations larger than his inclination to take things. He prefers to take things offered him and often wishes people on the street would offer him things so he can take them. Sometimes he suggests to people they offer him things so he can take them.

One day after he walks to the store and was still there, he meets someone he had met on the street. He has often thought of meeting this person on the street but he has never thought of meeting this person in the store. Jeremy forgets to tell his small joke when he gives the person working his money. Jeremy does not know why the person working does not laugh when Jeremy is given his change. All of this is very confusing. Jeremy and the person he met on the street walk out of the store. Jeremy thinks it will be less confusing if the person he met on the street and he meet on the street.

The person he met on the street is a good person to meet on the street and not a good person to meet in the store where the person working did not laugh. Jeremy suggested to the person he had met on the street when he had met the person he had met on the street the person he had met on the street offer him something he could take.

The person he had met on the street offers Jeremy the person he had met on the street. Jeremy took this person and became the person he had met on the street. This is one of the problems Jeremy had when he met someone he had met on the street in the store where the person working did not laugh when Jeremy was given his change.

Jeremy and the person he had met on the street are on the street. The person he had met on the street knows Jeremy knows the person he had met on the street since Jeremy had once become the person he had met on the street. Jeremy will have to take something from the person he had met on the street if the person he had met on the street offers him something to take. Jeremy does not like taking things from people he knows.

Sometimes Jeremy thinks it would be better if he were not on the street since he often wants to take things. He knows his inclination well and thinks if he is alone he will not think of taking things since he will not be offered things to take. If he is not going to be alone he prefers not to know the people who offer him things to take. He likes taking them so much he thinks he might take too much if he is offered too much. Jeremy is thinking the person he had met on the street will offer him something to take. He thinks if he suggests to the person he had met on the street the person he had met on the street offer him something to take Jeremy will take too much since he will be offered too much.

Jeremy knows the person he had met on the street knew Jeremy knew the person he had met on the street. Jeremy had thought of meeting the person he had met on the street on the street but he had not thought he would be confused. The person he had met on the street offered Jeremy too much. The person he had met on the street offered Jeremy so much Jeremy did not think he could take so much. The person he had met on the street offered Jeremy not so much and Jeremy took not so much.

Often Jeremy goes places other than the store on a walk. One day Jeremy meets the person he had met on the street at the museum.

Jeremy knows he knows the person he had met on the street

but Jeremy does not know if he knows the person he had met on the street at the museum. The person he had met on the street at the museum knows Jeremy. The person he had met on the street at the museum knows Jeremy so well the person he had met on the street at the museum offers Jeremy things he cannot take. The person he had met on the street at the museum offers Jeremy things Jeremy cannot see. Jeremy does not know if he is being offered things for him to take of if he is being offered things he cannot take since the person he had met on the street at the museum knows Jeremy does not like to take things from people he knows. The person he had met on the street at the museum might be a different person from the person he had met on the street. Jeremy thinks he can take things from the person he had met on the street at the museum since he does not know the person he had met on the street at the museum but Jeremy cannot see the things being offered. The person he had met on the street at the museum tells Jeremy the reason Jeremy cannot see the things being offered is that Jeremy does know the person he had met on the street at the museum. Jeremy thinks this is true.

At the museum Jeremy realizes he does not know the person he had met on the street at the museum. Jeremy does not know much other than what he has met on the street. Jeremy has always thought if someone was on the street and offered him something to take, Jeremy should take it. At the museum Jeremy cannot take things even if he thinks they are being offered to him. The person he had met on the street at the museum seems to be offering something he cannot take so Jeremy assumes he does not know this person.

Jeremy takes as much as he can from the person he had met on the street at the museum and Jeremy does not become the person he had met on the street at the museum. When Jeremy can take no more, the person he had met on the street at the museum suggests Jeremy offer something so the person he had met on the street at the museum can take it. Jeremy offers himself and the person he had met on the street at the museum becomes Jeremy.

The person who had become Jeremy and Jeremy walk together. They walk to the store to the museum to the park by the river. At the park by the river they stop and discuss how nice it is the person he had met on the street at the museum become Jeremy and Jeremy can be at the park by the river discussing their meeting. Jeremy or the person who has become Jeremy say how nice it is now no one has to suggest someone offer something so it can be taken by Jeremy. At the park by the river, Jeremy and the person who had become Jeremy become one. As one, they are no longer Jeremy and the person who had become Jeremy. They agree this is true.

Jeremy knows he cannot become one and the person who had become Jeremy cannot become Jeremy. Jeremy knows this since he had once become the person he had met on the street. This is Jeremy's secret which he does not tell to the person he had met on the street at the museum at the park by the river even after they had become one. The person he had met on the street at the museum at the park by the river become Jeremy and become one, of course, knows this.

The person he had met on the street in the store where the person working did not laugh when Jeremy was given his change at the museum become Jeremy at the park by the river and become one also knows it is impossible for Jeremy to take too much on an inclination.

JEREMY GOES TO MARKET

Jeremy can do no wrong. Wherever he goes, Fortune smiles her graciousness all about him. If Jeremy stubs his toe, as he bends over to rub it, he will find a dollar on the ground. If the company where he works goes bankrupt, Jeremy will have found a new job the week before. If a woman Jeremy has been seeing becomes pregnant, a paternity test will show Jeremy not to be the father. If the sky suddenly pours rain, Jeremy will hold a newly purchased umbrella.

On sunny days, Jeremy eats his lunch in the park across the street from the building where he works. Often he'll share his favorite bench with a particularly pretty woman who works for the same giant corporation as Jeremy. The two nibble on their sandwiches as they watch the sun dance across the glass face of the building which houses the giant corporation. The light bounces off the windows and illuminates areas in the park which the sun never illuminates by itself. The corporation brings light to the park and Jeremy and his friend bask in their company's reflected glory. The corporation casts a giant shadow as well, but Jeremy always finds the sunlight.

One day, as Jeremy walks along a corridor in the colossal building holding the giant corporation, he sees a man frowning. One of Jeremy's duties within the corporation is to know who is responsible for what among the very highly paid personnel in the giant building. Jeremy is not very highly paid himself, but he does know who does what among the very highly paid. It is possible Jeremy is not supposed to know as much as he does know, but that's one of the reasons Jeremy can do no wrong and Fortune smiles upon him.

"Why is this man frowning?" Jeremy asks himself and then he proceeds down the hall, to the elevator, down another hall, then to his desk.

Scanning numerous pieces of corporate information, memos, newsletters, press releases, annual reports, newspaper articles, Jeremy eventually discovers a reason which justifies to him why the man would be frowning. Jeremy places a phone call, and satisfied he has done the right thing, continues about his duties in the giant building and tells no one why he thinks the man was frowning.

Sitting in the park the next day, nibbing on their sandwiches, Jeremy mentions to the particularly pretty woman sitting next to him why he thinks the man was frowning.

"That's silly." says the particularly pretty woman and she continues nibbing upon her sandwich.

Jeremy explains to his friend what the frowning man is

responsible for in the giant corporation. Jeremy mentions all the research he completed the previous day and how he discovered why the frowning man was frowning.

"Look at the pretty light as it dances across the face of our building." says the particularly pretty woman.

Jeremy again explains how the frowning man is responsible for watching over the interests of the people working for the giant corporation. How the frowning man makes sure the older employees of the corporation, when they are replaced by younger, cheaper employees, own pieces of the giant corporation which they can trade for food and shelter as become even more old.

"See how our company's light brightens our park, and look," the particularly pretty woman gestures toward the city surrounding the park, "See how our company's light brings safety and clarity to all of our city. Without our company, our city would be in darkness." The particularly pretty woman turns her head and takes in all the areas of the city, receiving the reflected light from the glass face of the giant corporation's building.

Jeremy follows the reflected light and turns his head to view the sun on the glass of the building.

Without looking directly into the sun's reflection on the giant corporation's building, Jeremy feels the heat it produces on the skin of his face. Jeremy feels the warmth, closes his eyes and enjoys the comfort the light brings him. After a few moments, the heat on his face becomes uncomfortable and he opens his eyes to the reflection of the sun off the glass on the face of the giant corporation's building. Jeremy stares into the reflection of the sun for a brief moment. He knows if he stares much longer, his vision will be impaired. Jeremy knows if his vision is impaired, he may no longer be able to do no wrong and Fortune may smile elsewhere.

Once again Jeremy explains to the particularly pretty woman why the frowning man was frowning. Jeremy explains how he placed a call and hedged options on his piece of the giant corporation in case everyone involved with seeing that older workers of the giant corporation would be able to afford food and shelter as they got older began frowning as well.

"Feel how warm the sun is." says the particularly pretty woman.

Jeremy knows the particularly pretty woman isn't feeling how warm the sun is but only how warm the reflection of the sun is.

Jeremy also knows the building of the giant corporation casts an enormous shadow but Jeremy always manages to remain in the light so Fortune will at all times smile upon him and he can do no wrong.

Later that same week, Jeremy reads a memo which says the frowning man has left the giant corporation and moved to another giant corporation where he will be even more appreciated than he is at Jeremy's giant corporation. The corporation thanks the frowning man for his years of vital work and wishes him well in his future endeavors. Jeremy places more phone calls and speaks with people he hasn't spoken with in years.

Jeremy does not eat lunch in his usual spot this day and instead visits with old acquaintances in other giant corporations.

Two weeks later, Jeremy and the particularly pretty woman again sit on Jeremy's favorite bench in the park across the street from the building of the giant corporation where they both work, nibbling on their sandwiches. Jeremy tells the particularly pretty woman that he soon will be leaving the giant corporation and moving to another giant corporation where his work will be more appreciated and he will be paid more money. He explains to the particularly pretty woman that all the people in the department where the frowning man once worked are now frowning as well. Jeremy mentions how, that even though at the present time the giant corporation's rules prohibit Jeremy from selling any of the bits and pieces of the company which he owns, he has purchased "shorts" which guarantee him that if the price of his bits and pieces of the giant corporation become less valuable, his "shorts" will protect his investment in the company and guarantee at least part of the monies he is planning on trading for food and lodging when whichever giant corporation eventually replaces him with a younger, cheaper version of himself. Jeremy explains all this to the particularly pretty woman twice.

"When the days get warmer, perhaps I'll wear shorts too." The particularly pretty woman tilts her face into the light of the reflected sun echoing from the face of the giant corporation's building.

Three weeks later, as Jeremy is still rearranging the work space in his new cubicle, he reads how his former giant corporation has gotten into trouble owing to accounting irregularities. He reads how the price of the various bits and pieces of the giant corporation have fallen drastically in value. He reads how the older present, and the older former, employees of the giant corporation have lost most of the value of the bits and pieces which they owned and were going to trade for food and lodging as they got even older. Jeremy reads how some of the present and past high salaried people may be going to jail.

Jeremy is thankful he made the phone call when he saw the frowning man frown.

Jeremy thinks of the particularly pretty woman and all his former fellow workers and hopes for the best.

Jeremy knows he can do no wrong and Fortune will always smile upon him.

Jeremy continues rearranging his new cubicle.